Blood Lust

Tanisha Parekh

BLUEROSE PUBLISHERS
India | U.K.

Copyright © Tanisha Parekh 2025

All rights reserved by author. No part of this publication may be reproduced, stored in a retrieval system or transmitted in any form or by any means, electronic, mechanical, photocopying, recording or otherwise, without the prior permission of the author. Although every precaution has been taken to verify the accuracy of the information contained herein, the publisher assumes no responsibility for any errors or omissions. No liability is assumed for damages that may result from the use of information contained within.

BlueRose Publishers takes no responsibility for any damages, losses, or liabilities that may arise from the use or misuse of the information, products, or services provided in this publication.

For permissions requests or inquiries regarding this publication, please contact:

BLUEROSE PUBLISHERS
www.BlueRoseONE.com
info@bluerosepublishers.com
+91 8882 898 898
+4407342408967

ISBN: 978-93-6783-010-9

Cover Design: Shubham
Typesetting: Sagar

First Edition: January 2025

Acknowledgement

Writing this novel has been an incredible journey, and I could not have completed it without the support, guidance, and encouragement of many remarkable people.

First and foremost, I would like to thank [Piyush Singh & Kavya Parekh], whose unwavering belief in me and my work has been a constant source of inspiration. Their patience, feedback, and dedication to helping me refine my vision have been invaluable.

To my family and friends, thank you for your endless love and support. Your understanding during the long hours I spent writing and your willingness to listen to my ideas, no matter how far-fetched, kept me going when I needed it most.

I am deeply grateful to [BlueRose publications], whose expert insight and meticulous attention to detail elevated this story in ways I couldn't have done alone. Your guidance has made all the difference.

Lastly, to the readers who pick up this book: thank you for your time, your imagination, and for allowing me to share my story with you. Your support means the world to me.

This book is as much yours as it is mine.

Chapter 1

'Finally this long day is over.' I pull into my driveway after a long, tiring day of work and turn the car off.

I look at myself in the visor mirror fixing hair and lipstick before getting out of the car.

I walk to my front door and unlock it, excited to see my boyfriend, James.

He's been sending me texts all day about the dirty things he wants to do to me tonight, and after this long day I've been looking forward to it.

I can't stop thinking about how I want his hands all over every inch of my body. I want to tug his beautiful brown locks while he makes me shiver with pleasure.

I unlock the door and walk inside.

"Baby! You're home!" James my boyfriend, gets off the couch and stumbles towards me. When he gets close enough, I can smell the alcohol on him.

'He's drunk! Again!'

James tries to lean in and kiss me. This isn't what I had been expecting.

James goes in for the kiss, his eyes are bloodshot and hungry. I place my hands on his chest and push him away.

I'm not in the mood anymore.

"OH, come on, baby." He tries to kiss me again. He's so drunk, he can't even tell that I'm annoyed with him.

"James! Stop."

"Jeez, what's your problem?" I ignore his question and walk around him, further into my home.

I notice it's a complete mess in here. There's James's food wrappers, plastic cups, beer cans and dirty clothes littered around.

"You couldn't clean up a little while I was at work today?"

"I was going to, but I...forgot."

'Jeez, he just forgot?'

"Look at this place, there's so much mess everywhere."

"I just don't let it bother me." James tries to approach me again, but I move around him and start walking around the room picking up some of his trash.

'I hope he feels bad seeing me pick up after him.' "Clearly"

"I was too busy thinking about having you in my arms."

"And that's supposed to make it okay?" I give up cleaning, start heading down the hallway towards the bedroom. James follows me, still stumbling and slurring his words.

"I'll do it later."

I scoff as I know James always promises to do things but never completes them.

"Come on, Claire, don't be like this." I stay silent throughout the walk to my room as James follows me. At this point, I just need to be away from him.

'Maybe I'll just take a nice hot bubble bath with some wine after all this.'

James stands near the bedroom with his hands folded staring right at me, as if he wants me to hurry up.

"Claire?" 'I hope he's about to apologize to me.' "Yeah?"

"What's for dinner? I'm starving "'He's unbelievable'

"James, please.... working all day long and coming home to see this mess is enough, I don't have the energy to cook for you anymore, and you didn't do anything all day long."

James sighs and acts as if the allegations I put on him were false.

"You're right. I'm the problem and you're Ms Perfect!" I stand there in disbelief as James chooses to play victim and puts all the blame on me.

"I'm sorry. I'd just like to come home after work and relax instead of cooking and picking up after you."

"And I'd like you to come home and not immediately start bitching at me. But I guess we can't always get what we want."

"That's not fair! If I am going to be the only one making a living, I do expect you to help me out with the chores."

"Don't be ridiculous. Making money isn't always everything. "

"Why haven't you tried getting a job yet? And if you loved me, you would help me not to feel so stressed when I get home."

"Your job is not even that hard. Come talk to me when you're working a better job" 'He just did not said that!'

I raise my hand and slap him across the face, outraged and unable to stop myself.

James recoils and gasps, he stands there and stares at me. He's wearing a stunned expression.

"Do not ever say that to me again, James."

James touches his reddening cheek where I slapped him. I know I shouldn't have done it, but I just couldn't help my reaction.

'I'm not going to apologize. My job is hard enough! He doesn't know what it's like. '

James gives me a disappointed glare, then turns and walk out of the room.

***

I and James sit on the opposite corners of the room. Ready for night after this hateful night.

Suddenly, James's phone starts vibrating, I see him pull it out of his pocket. He reads the name on his screen and stands up.

"James!? Where are you going?" Without answering my question James slams the door behind him.

Two hours pass by and there's no sign of James getting back home. I walk to my bathroom and get ready for bed.

'It's not like him to stay out this late.' I plop myself back down in front of the TV, but I'm restless and constantly glancing out the window.

"Never mind! I could use this time for better things." I go to my favourite corner in the house: my bookshelf. "Reading always make me feel better."

I scan the spines, trailing the books with my pointer finger. I love to read before bed.

I love being able to escape into a world that is not my own. It's comforting to me.

"Wait, this book..." I see a book I hadn't noticed before. It's ancient-looking, made of leather, and embossed with gold.

Even though I don't quite recognize it, something about the book feels familiar to me.

"Have I seen this somewhere before?"

I'm about to pull it off the shelf. I feel some sort of connection to it, and I can't figure out why.

I look at the title. It's called Vampire Histories.

"Vampires?" I start flipping through the pages. Quickly I become captivated by the contents. It's sexy, dark, and mysterious. "How are all vampires so hot?" I read a couple of titbits about vampires: how they live off of human blood. How they're forever living masters of seduction. "And what is this city? It looks so beautiful!" I keep turning pages until a ray of sunlight streams in from the small window in the room.

I can't believe the sun is rising already. I stayed up all night. At the same moment the sunlight spreads over the vampire book, it flies out of my hands and onto the ground. "What the hell?" I stare at the book. It's vibrating in a supernatural way.

Before I can even process what's happening, the book flies open to the middle pages. "Oh my gosh!" The centre of the book is glowing! I'm terrified, but I feel drawn towards it. Words are glittering off the page.

Something in me is telling me to read them out loud even though it's a language I don't recognize. Somehow, I'm able to pronounce the words perfectly and clearly. "Venitadlucen. Intra in undo notum..."

The world around me falls away. I feel my feet lift off the ground. I want to scream, but I can't. I'm pulled further and further away. Away from my house. Away from James. Away from the world I've always known.

Suddenly I'm thrown into a mysterious world. There are so many Questions arising in the back of my Mind. But it all seems too much to take in and I can't help but look around in awe at this place. "What is this Place?"

***

I'm in the woods. But something is different about these woods. It's as if the trees are twinkling. The night air and cool breeze on my skin feel almost hypnotizing. Everything around me seems a little hazy. I struggle to wake up and get on my feet.

My eyes fall to my feet and I scream. A beautiful man is lying on the ground at my feet! Who is he? It's late, dark, and ominous here in this mysterious forest. I'm incredibly confused with no idea how I could have ended up here that I'm almost too distracted to remember the handsome, seemingly unconscious man lying at my feet.

"Hey. Are you okay?" I kneel beside the man. Looking over his taut, muscular body. I spot some gashes and deep wounds which are bleeding profusely, the red stains spreading across his pressed shirt and pants.

"Hey, can you hear me?" The man doesn't move, and he doesn't open his eyes. He looks so peaceful and serene that it almost seems as if he's just sleeping. I can't help but stare at his beauty. How is it even possible for anyone to be so attractive? He doesn't even seem real....

I could go on staring at him for hours. But if I don't do something to help him, he might not make it. "Oh my god, what do I do? Think, Think! What did I learn in my EMT training? I know I can help him!"

I lean down and press my ear against his chest. It's hard to determine if the heart I hear beating in his or my own. "Oh my gosh!" Being this close to him I can see how perfectly carved his face is. He's so beautiful it seems unreal. "Okay, Focus!" I pull myself away from his chest and stare at him. 'If his chest is rising and falling, then that means he's alive and breathing.

I'm terrified about all the blood he's losing, but I've been trained for this...I continue to observe him and notice that his chest is rising and falling. "He's alive!"

I put my hands over his body and hold him, trying to bring him back to consciousness but my hands freeze as they hover over his wounds. "What the..."I watch as the bloodstains that were spreading across his shirt slowly fade away. It's as if the time is reversing. 'What is happening?' The man's eyes snap open.

"You're awake!" Relief floods me, but just for a moment. Instead of yelling out in pain or begging me to help him, the men smiles at me.

When he grins, I notice his sharp and menacing fangs. 'He's not human!' I scream and jump back. I realize that this man is dangerous. 'Whoever attacked him must have done it in self-defence!' I turn and begin running. 'Why isn't he chasing me?'

I look over my shoulder and see the man getting to his feet as he stares at me with a look of amusement on his face. 'My house...the book... That man is....a vampire.'

Right when I think he's going to leave me alone and I'm going to escape out of these woods, I hear a whooshing sound. "Somebody, please help me!"

The vampire grabs me and pins me against a tree. "Did you really think you'd be able to escape so easily?"

Chapter 2

I am powerless against a vampire. There is no way I am going to be able to escape him. The man pulls me closer by the waist and whispers in my ear... "Not so easily..." His hands travel to my neck and then to my jawline, he slightly lifts my chin making me face him.

"Are you going to kill me?"

"If I was, I would have done it already." I gulp questioning whether or not I should believe him. "Then what do you want from me? I don't have anything to offer you."

The vampire stares at me intensely, and I feel myself longing for him, unable to process my thoughts. I nervously wait for the vampire to speak guessing it's going to be a threatening statement, but then the vampire's gaze softens.

"I don't want anything from you. I'm not going to hurt you." I go to scream again, but he holds up his hand to stop me. "I am not going to hurt you. You have my word."

"Then why did you just pin me?"

"I couldn't help myself. You just..."

"I just what?" 'Why am I not afraid? I'm alone in the woods with an actual vampire for God's sake!'

The vampire then takes a deep breath not breaking eye contact. "Allow me to introduce myself. My name is Alex. Son of Lord Eden"

"Okay, Alex. Mind telling me where the hell am I?"

Alex chuckles. "You, my dear, have found yourself in Night City."

I think back about the old leather- bound book. The name doesn't sound super familiar, but I'm guessing there's information about him in the book that somehow leads me here.

"Am I supposed to know who Lord Eden is?"

"Lord Eden? He's the greatest and, as some would say, the most powerful vampire to ever exist."

"Are there others like you?"

"Yes a lot of them." As I stand in the middle of the woods with Alex, suddenly there's a rustling in the bushes behind, making me jump in fright. Alex comes closer to me. For some reasons, I feel calm. "You are safe with me...." "It's Claire."

"Claire. How beautiful." When Alex takes my name, it feels like a melody to my ears. The sense of comfort washes over me as I continue feeling more and safer in his presence. 'I haven't even let my guard down, yet he makes me feel some sort of way like, I could trust him? No! What's wrong with my thoughts?! It must be his magical vampire powers.'

Alex holds his arm out to me waiting for me to take it. "Shall we?"

"I am not going anywhere with you until you answer some questions." Alex smiles

"What would you like to know?"

"Do you have a family, other than your father? Do you have a girlfriend? Is gallivanting around the woods late at night a favourite hobby of yours? Are you here hunting for blood to drink?"

Alex seems amused by my questions but not hesitant to answer them. It's clear that he is patient with me. Alex takes his sweet time to answer my questions and simultaneously glances over at me. My eyes meet his multiple times and I feel a spark fly.

"Yes, I do have a family. No girlfriend. I don't gallivant. But I do enjoy my Nightly walks."

"Is night City... a magical place?"

"If by magical you mean full of other magical creatures and beings, then yes." Another wave of fear washes over me, but Alex gives me a kind smile, and it makes me feel better.

"Maybe he really will protect me." I and Alex continue talking, asking each other questions, and giving each other vague answers. I'm not one hundred percent convinced I can trust him yet. "You're not giving me honest detailed answers." "Neither are you."

"Because I know you're just asking to be polite, who could've thought, I would be here be here asking questions to a vampire getting to know him."

"You will learn a lot more about me, in no time." Alex holds his arm out to me again. "Where do you want to take me?"

"I will walk you home, of course"

"But I don't know how to get home let alone I don't even know how I got here." I start babbling and freaking out. Alex reaches out and places a comforting hand on my shoulder. A tingling sensation shoots right through me. I don't want him to take his hand away. "It will be alright, Claire. What is the last thing you remember?"

"Reading a book back at my house. Then the next thing I know, I'm here..... Alex, do you know anything about a book called Vampire Histories? Do you know how it could have caused me to be....transported here?" Alex appears as if he is in deep thoughts for a long while. Them he finally speaks.

"I am Afraid I don't."

"I'm scared, Alex." Alex takes his hand off of me. He appears to be thinking about what the best solution is. Tears start forming in my eyes. I'm scared I am never going to find my way back. "I don't feel safe here. I just want to go back home."

"I am sorry I don't know how to help you get back to....your world. But come with me. You can stay the night at my place. In the morning we can assess the situation with a refreshed mind." There's a rustling in the bushes again, and Alex squints at something over my shoulder, jumping into fight mode.

"It's not safe for you out here. You'll feel much better once we get to my home."

'I don't know if I should trust him. But I don't want to be in these woods anymore, either." Alex stays close to me, as he offers me his arm, I take it and hold it tightly as we begin walking out of the woods.

"What was it that attacked you?"

"An ogre. They roam all around these woods."

"Why would it attack you though?" I shudder at the thought of what a real-life ogre might look like.

"The big ole brute just felt like picking a fight. He must have been bored." My eyes widen in fear, and Alex Smiles. I question how he is so calm about it but then he speaks. "As I said, you have nothing to fear when I'm with you." I find myself moving even closer to him. Alex notices it, and his eyes go to my hand that is tightly clutching onto him.

"It's not far from here." I and Alex eventually get out of the woods and enter the town. As I walk, I notice all kind of mystical creatures. "I must be dreaming. There is no way they're all real! How can this be happening?"

I look around at everyone and everything questioning this alternate reality. Alex catches me stunned at the surroundings and finally breaks the silence. "What's the matter? You act as you've never seen a leprechaun before." I am passing a small man in a green hat with a red beard and long hair. He stops what he was working on and is staring at Alex with a look of respect. As I keep walking, I notice that all around me, every creature has stopped to watch Alex...and me.

"Alex, do you and your family.....rule the land?"

"As I said, you'll learn a lot more about me with time."

'Why doesn't he give me any honest and true answers?' As I continue walking, I can't help but look back and forth between the creatures and Alex. Some of them are staring at me, too. 'Do they pity me? Do they think I have fallen for his trap and am about to be lured to my death?' I look at Alex again. He's so muscular, manly, and confident. Something about him makes me feel as if he wouldn't hurt me, but if he did I might....Like it.

I and Alex continue walking along the cobblestone-paved road curves. Ahead of me is a large castle up on a hill, and it seems to look over the entire city. "Is that where we're headed?"

"Yes. Welcome to my home, Claire." I gulp. It's beautiful and mysterious and slightly ominous.

***

I approach the main gates, Alex opens them and lets me across the threshold. He then locks the gate behind me. 'There's no turning back now.'

I'm in complete awe as Alex walks me through the castle. I feel as if I'm in some sort of trance. And being in Alex's castle, where he feels at home, I notice how much more relaxed he seems. It only makes me want to stare at him more. 'What is it about him....?'

Alex stops walking with me when I get to a certain hallway. He motions to two doors. One is further down the hall, and one is closer to the grand staircase. "Take your pick."

"That one down there, please."

"Very well." He leads me down the hall to the room I have selected. He opens the door and the two of us step inside.

As beautiful as the room is, I'm still uncomfortable and overwhelmed. 'I just can't believe this is actually happening to me!'

"Is this to your liking?"

"Yes. Thank you." Alex points to the wardrobe on the other side of the room. "There are some clothes in there. Pick out whatever you'll be most comfortable to sleep in. Anything you want. "He leaves, and I go and open the wardrobe.

"Wow, I look irresistible in this. This will make Alex unable to take his eyes off of me!" After I finish getting changed, there's a knock on the door. I go to answer it. Alex is back. The first thing he does is gaze at me intensely. Maybe even longingly, it's hard for me to be sure. "I just wanted to make sure you were getting settled in okay."

"I am. Thank you for letting me stay here." 'Oh my god, he looks even sexier in his nightwear. How is that possible?'

"I can still sense there's something you're not telling me." He walks over to the grand bed in my room and sits on the edge of it. Then he motions for me to do the same. "You can tell me what's on your mind. I want to help make sure you're comfortable." I bite my lower lip and look into his eyes. 'I can't believe how kind he is. Is this all an act, or can I really trust a vampire?'

I sigh and tell him about all of my concerns and discomfort. He silently listens and nods his head along. He is good at telling me comforting words and giving me thoughtful advice. 'How is he so easy to talk to?' "Anyway, I'm sure you don't want to sit here and listen to me all night."

Alex places a hand on my knee. I feel a heat radiated from him and crawls up my thigh. It makes me lean in closer to him. "I promise you, Claire, everything will feel much better in the morning."

I stare at his lips. They're red and so vividly contrast against his pale skin. I wonder what it would feel like to kiss him. I instantly snap out of my thoughts and focus on Alex. Alex then takes his hand off of me, and it saddens me.

He motions to a door in my room that I hadn't noticed before. "You even picked the room connected to mine. So, I will be right through there if you need anything at all." I nod my head. I'm very grateful, but still very shaken up and worried. Alex seems to notice this about me. He moves closer to me on the bed.

I get the sense that he wants to comfort me. He reaches out and takes my hand in his. I notice how perfectly my hands fit together. 'This doesn't feel anything like holding James's hand.'

Alex's hand is big and strong. And his touch makes me feel much more relaxed. 'Gosh, what is it that I'm feeling?' Alex seems to sense this, and his head leans in towards me. The air is thick with tension, and I can feel just how much my body wants him. I want to know what makes me feel this way.

I know it's wrong to fantasize about him whereas he's just helping me but I can't help it. There is no denying the chemistry between us. 'I don't know if I am going to be able to resist him....'

Alex leans in, but I turn my head just in time. Alex pauses, his lips lingering centimetres away from my skin. I want to turn back. 'But I can't do that to James.' My skin sizzles where his lips should've been long after he pulls away from me. "Goodnight, Claire."

"Goodnight, Alex." Alex heads over to my bedroom door. He opens it and goes to leave, but before he does, he stops himself and looks back at one last time giving me a sexy devilish grin. "This...is going to be very interesting time for me to practice my self-control." He then leaves before I can say anything back, He closes the door and I lay on my back, my heart pounding 'Alex worries about being able to control himself around me? Me? A sexy, hot, dangerous vampire wants me. And I want him, too....'

"That makes two of us, Alex."

Chapter 3

I'm lying wide awake in bed at night, unable to sleep. Alex knocks on the door connected to my bedroom. He enters with his hands tucked inside his pocket. 'He's back!' Alex is beautiful and smouldering. It appears as if some kind of steam is radiating off of him.

I gaze at him longingly from over in my bed. "What are you doing here?"

"I couldn't sleep. I had to see you." *Desire fills me. Alex uses his super speed and is suddenly at my bedside. He throws my covers off pulling me closer to him. Then in a split second Alex flips me over making me sit on top of him.*

'Why is he so fucking hot? How is one supposed to resist him?' Alex flashes me his fangs. It briefly crosses my mind that maybe I am supposed to be alarmed, But I am not.

"Alex..." *I take his name in a soft seducing way. Pleased, Alex moves in super speed again, his fangs at my throat. I think he's going to bite me, but that doesn't scare me. Instead of his teeth sinking into my flesh, Alex presses his lips against my skin. Softly at first. He trails the kisses down my neck.*

His hands explore their way as I throw my head back in Pleasure.

I let out a moan tugging on his silky hair wanting more. Alex stops for a split second and looks me in the eye. "Do you want me to stop...?"

I'm as full of lust and desire as I feel my core throbbing, but I know this isn't a good idea. "Yes, I guess we should stop." Alex scoffs.

"What if I don't want to?" I arch my back so that I can be closer to his body. I trail my hands to his chest signalling him to keep going. "I don't want you to, either. I'm just trying to behave."

"I like when you're naughty." Alex resumes as he shifts his gaze from my eyes to my lips making it super hard to control myself. He then leads his hand to the hem of my Nightdress, gently moving it further. I take a deep breath wanting more. He pulls away.

"Why are you stopping?" Frustrated, I sit up grabbing at his nightshirt ripping it, not caring about the buttons flying off. "Alex!" Alex grunts in pleasure. He loves to see my dominant side.

"It feels so good to finally have you in my arms."

There's a knock on my door, and I snap my eyes open. I had only been dreaming. Before I can say anything, the door opens, and a women dressed in a maid's uniform come bustling inside.

She's older and appears to have a lot of energy. "Good morning, I've been sleeping for hours!"

"I have?" 'Oh my god, I was dreaming? Why was I thinking of all that? Something's wrong with me but it felt so real!'

"It's late! You really ought to get up and freshen up. There will be breakfast down the stairs."

I look at myself, confused for a moment as to where I am and how I got here. Then everything comes back to me. The book. The mysterious glow from it. How I left my house and James behind.... Then I feel myself blush as I think about the dream. "Sorry."

"Not to worry dear. You needed your rest."

'I can't stop thinking about Alex. I shouldn't think all this it's wrong.' "Where is Alex?"

"Oh you'll be seeing him. He has a wonderful day planned for you. We've been preparing all morning."

"Really?"

"Alex will take great care of you. We all will. I promise."

I like this women and her calming presence. For the first time since arriving here, I feel completely safe. "Well then, thank you."

"I was wondering if you need help with anything." I stand, ready to help clean the room and change the sheets. I'm not used to someone else cleaning.

"My dear girl, all I need is for you to get ready for breakfast!" I and the maid continue to make small talk while I freshen up. The maid leaves my room, closing the door on her way out. I finally get to see the dress options she sets out for me.

'What should I wear?' That's when one of the gowns catches my eye, it looks like it is made out of pure silk with such intricate details. I instantly feel happy with the thought of wearing it. I wear a cotton dress and take a look at myself in the mirror.

I thank the maid and put on the slippers she provided, walking out into the hall.

I turn left down the hall. It's long and winding. 'Where am I taking myself?' I explore as it's quite and empty for a moment. But then I turn a corner and see more castle workers, all of them craning their necks to look at me. These aren't human castle workers. They are creatures of all kinds. They're all in different shapes, sizes, and colours.

'Why do they seen so foreign, yet so familiar? Have I read fairy tales about them before?' Some of them are vampires, as well. I can tell by their paleness.

I smile at them kindly and continue walking down the hall. I come across bright open windows and paintings. The paintings are unique but creepy. I see a staircase, so I make my way to breakfast. I look around at all of the servants.

"Can somebody point me to the dining hall?" The servants fight over who gets to escort me to breakfast. A creature with a human torso and a horse body wins, and he takes me gently the elbow to a grand, beautifully designed dining room with mahogany- panelled walls and an intricately designed chandelier.

He pulls out a chair at the end of the dining table. I sit down. In front of me I'd a massive assortment of breakfast foods, crackers, coffee, tea, milk, and water.

"Oh my god, Is this all for me?"

The maid has entered the room again.

"Of course, it is!"

"It looks delicious!" More castle servants make their way into the dining room. They all want to talk to me. I smile and nod and wave to them one by one. My stomach is growling and I would love to eat, but I don't want to be rude. 'They must have visitors very often....'

"Can't you all just leave her alone? Go on! Get to work. There's much to be done!"

The creatures leave. "Sorry about them, Dear, They are just very taken with you."

"Why?" She pushes my chair in and pats my shoulder. "Eat up." She turns and leaves.

I'm nibbling on a croissant when Alex walks into the dining room. An invisible breeze is blowing his hair back, and he looks relaxed and refreshed and even more devastatingly handsome than he did last night. It appears that he has fully healed.

"Good morning, Claire! Glad to see you awake!"

'Oh god, how am I supposed to look at him normally after the dream I had last night.' I'm having a hard time not picturing him naked and thinking the dream. "Good morning, Alex."

"Did you sleep well?"

"Yes, thank you. It's really kind of you to let me stay here."

"We're happy to have you. As you could probably tell." He's vibrant and joyful and excited as he moves and sits across from me at the far end of the twenty- person table. "Yeah, all of your workers seemed very happy to see me for some reason."

"Yes, I could hear them when I was upstairs getting ready! So, I was thinking."

"Yes?"

"I have a proposal for you."

"A proposal?"

"Yes. Well, let me start off by saying, I would like to give you a better answer to the question you asked me last night." I wait. "I don't rule the city. Yet, I am actually running to be the leader of Night City."

"That's great! You would do wonderfully."

"Yes, I hope to modernize everything a bit and give this city the rejuvenation I feel it needs."

"Is anybody running against you?" Alex takes a deep breath it almost seems like the question is making him uncomfortable. "My brother...." I raise my eyebrows and nod, still not understanding the reason the two brothers are running against each other.

Alex turns to look at me almost making me gasp at his beautiful sight. "I know it will be too much to ask but having you by my side would really help me out in the biggest election. I promise to make my stay better and until you go home can you help me out?" Alex's sincere tone makes it impossible to resist the offer.

"I've been wanting to see the city during the day!" Alex looks surprised by my answer. "Really? You'll come with me?"

"Of course! It's the least I could do since you let me stay here."

"Well! This is great news. And I assure you. I'm going to get you home as soon as humanly possible. It's just going to take me some time to do some research." I feel in my bones that I can trust him. Alex has taken great care of me so far. I offer him a kind smile. "Thank you."

Alex tells me to finish eating and freshen up. Apparently, he has a surprise for me as a thank you for helping him. 'What could the surprise possibly be?' My mind is racing with so many thoughts, I can't stop thinking about Alex. The way he makes me feel is ecstatic and being around him always puts my mind at rest.

I take two bites of my croissant, one sip of my orange juice. Then I push out my chair and eagerly start walking back. "Done eating already?" "I was wondering how you felt about the flowers I planned just outside." All of the servants still want to talk to me. Warmth floods through me at their kindness.

I feel important here, and the adrenaline starts pulsating through my veins. "I'm sorry, I can't talk right now!" I race up the stairs to get changed and ready for the day.

After I finish getting ready in my room, I walk back down the grand staircase and enter the foyer where Alex is waiting for me. 'I can't believe this is actually happening.' Alex smiles at me and it makes my heart melt. "You look stunning." I feel myself blushing and don't reply. He takes my hand and signals me to follow him somewhere.

"I have something to show you." I blush, even more, thinking again of the dream. He seems to notice this. "I can see the blood rising in your cheeks. Are you alright?"

"Sorry." Alex laughs. "Don't apologize. You can't help that. You're human. And that you smell so good."

He leads me through the castle, and I walk out of French double doors onto a beautiful terrace. There's a fountain and flowers all around, as well as a beautiful, ornate bench and twinkling lights.

I see a balcony with a wrought iron railing, and the two of us walk over to it. From up here on the terrace, I can see all of The Night City.

It is simply breath-taking to look at, and I can't help but gasp. "This is beautiful."

"You like it?"

"I'm speechless, Alex."

Alex smiles. Then he points at something. "Do you see the castle over there?" I follow his finger and notice a second castle across the way. It looks gothic, dark and ominous.

Nothing like the light, airy, modern one that I are currently standing outside of. "I see it."

"That is my brother's castle." I take in the city and other castle and the beautiful greenery, and I'm beside myself.

I'm overwhelmed and I feel on top of the world. I don't understand why. "This is insane."

"I'm glad you're enjoying yourself." I look back over at Alex's brother castle. 'What kind of vampire is he?' The thought of him being dangerous and not liking humans sends a shiver up my spine.

"Are you cold?" Alex steps closer to me. "Oh no. I'm fine. Thank you."

"You're shivering." I don't want to admit that I am uneasy about His brother's castle. "I guess I'm a little bit cold."

"Do you need a jacket?"

"No, That's OK." He places his hands on my shoulders. "I can warm you up." He starts gently rubbing small circles on my bare shoulder blades, and more Goosebumps erupt across my entire body.

He steps even closer to me, to where his chest is almost touching my back. I turn around and throw my arms over Alex's shoulder. Without another thought, I press my lips against his.

It feels so good that I can't help but kiss him even deeper. Alex resists at first, only in surprise. Then he grabs onto my lower back and pulls me into him as his tongue enters my mouth. "Fuck! I should have known this is how a kiss with you would feel." I and Alex stand there and make out for what feels like hours.

'This feels good on levels I can't even explain.' My first kiss with Alex was exactly how I had imagined, he was soft and held me extremely close to him. I had to stand on my tippy-toes to match with his height and he seems to enjoy it too.

"Can't get enough?" I almost don't think I'd care if he were to have his way with me on the terrace, the whole town watching. In fact, I might enjoy that. A small moan escapes my lips thinking about it.

"Ah! Alex...." Alex bites my bottom lip, just enough to where it hurts a little, but not enough to pierce my skin. I claw the back of his neck as he steps away.

"We should stop before I get too carried away." Alex flashes me a genuine smile moving a piece of hair strand away from my face.

I stand shoulder to shoulder with Alex and look out from the terrace. Just as I am about to ask him a question, I feel a presence behind me.

Chapter 4

I turn and see a purple, goblin- like man giving Alex a hard look. "Master, you are needed in the study. It's urgent. I'm sorry to interrupt you.

Alex turns to me, looking disappointed. "I'm sorry Claire. It shouldn't be too long. Make yourself at home." Alex races away with his servant.

***

I leave the terrace and enter the castle again. I walk for a bit before I notice a human woman strolling past me, down the corridor. She hasn't seen me. "Who is that?" Being sneaky, I decide to quietly follow behind the women to see where she's headed. s=She turns a corner and goes up a small staircase. 'Where is she going?'

I head up the stairs and continue to follow her, careful to hide behind statues and pillars. The woman turns another corner, and I'm about to follow her, but then a hand on my shoulder stops me. "Claire, there you are. You should get back to your room."

"My room?" Alex has a hard look on his face.

"It's the safest there. I just don't want anything to happen to you. Just stay in your room and I will get you soon. I swear." I look at his hand on my shoulder.

I love how small I feel under his firm grasp. I wish he would come to my bedroom with me. "Okay, I'll go." He nods at me before turning and walking off again.

I go back to my room and lock my door. I sit on my bed for a moment, but I am too antsy to wait around all day. I don't know what else to do, so I start digging through my dresser and armoire drawers, trying to find something interesting. "Even a book would be nice to read."

'I'm inside a giant castle with so much to see, and I can't go anywhere? How boring!' I pace around the room trying to find a way back. I love being in this beautiful town but me still miss home.

I have too many thoughts running through my brain and too much pent-up energy from the tension between me and Alex. As much as I trust him, there's still a part of me that believes finding a way back alone is key. I lay back on my bed and leave a sigh.

'Alex is all I can think about. His handsome expressions. The way he touches me. The way I feel every time I'm around him. How strong and fast he is. Everything he does is fascinating to me.' "This is not it, snap out of it, Claire!" I push myself out of bed determined to go talk to all the workers and gather information.

'I won't be able to think about anything else until I solve this problem....'

I quickly walk down the grand staircase and find a worker who could possibly know something. The worker quickly excuses herself from the assigned work and greets me.

"Hello, how may I help you?"

"This may sound weird but are you aware of where I came from?"

"I'm afraid I don't! Alex didn't tell us about that."

"I know and now I'm not able to ask anyone for help since nobody seems to know anything about my world." The worker looks at me in utter confusion but her facial expressions quickly change as she seems to remember something.

"The city is filled with magic my love, you should consult the town's great sorcerers for your concern."

'Sorcerers? Where will I find them?' Before I could ask the worker another question she excuses herself. 'At least I found out something.' I take a deep breath and let myself get the worries out of my head for a while, that's when Alex's thoughts flood my mind. 'He never really leaves my mind, huh.'

Before I can even go all the way through the stairs, I hear a commotion coming from the room next to mine. "That's Alex's room." I freeze ad wait to see if I hear anything else. Then I jump when a large thud sounds. "Alex!" Worried, I race to the door that connects my room with his. 'Oh god, please let him be okay.' I swing open the door.

Getting a clearer look in Alex's room makes me gasp in horror. Alex is at the end of his bed, leaning over it. "Alex?" Alex doesn't even hear me. There lies a women on the foot of the bed. The same women I saw walking in castle earlier.

Alex has his teeth sunk into her neck, and blood is pouring out of her. He is feeding off of her! "Oh my god, what should I do?"

Chapter 5

I am standing in the doorway of Alex's bedroom. He is so consumed by drinking the blood of the women I saw earlier in the hallway that he doesn't even notice me when I gasp aloud. 'I don't think he would want me to be here and watch this happen...'

I grab the handle and close the door enough so that it's only open a crack. I can't make out anything the women is saying because the room is so large and the massive king bed is against the far wall. 'Is he hurting her?'

I see the way the gorgeous blonde women is moving around on the bed, gripping Alex's royal blue bedspread tightly with both of her hands. Her eyes might be closed, but I'm not sure.

I hear Alex make a noise of pure pleasure. Heat rises inside of myself as I watch. 'I don't know if it's because I'm watching something I am not supposed to, or because of the way Alex and the women are acting while he drinks from her, but oh my gosh, this is incredibly sexy.'

The women lets out a moan, and Alex tightens his grip on her tousled hair. My heart starts pounding. 'Why am I wishing I was her right now?' There is blood dripping from Alex's mouth and the women's neck, but I'm not bothered by it. If anything, it's just making me more turned on.

I'm throbbing between my legs, watching them. "Alex, oh my god, YES!" Hearing her scream of ecstasy makes a moan escape my lips. It's loud enough that Alex hears me and whips his head around.

Alex bears his fangs as blood covers his mouth and trails down his neck onto his tailored shirt. He is breathing fast. "I'm sorry!" The women opens her eyes and jumps up when she sees me. Alex has a crazed look in his eyes.

I barely have time to think as he uses his super- speed and races towards me. I quickly head to my bedroom door but he stops me. 'He's furious with me!' Alex reaches me in no time at all. He grabs my shoulders and I feel myself flying.

Alex pushes me up against my bedroom dresser, his eyes full of anger. His blood- stained mouth in inches from me. "Haven't you heard of knocking?"

"I-I thought you were in trouble." I'm afraid of him now. I remember that I hardly know him, even if it feels like I do. 'He could kill me in an instant!'

Alex's hand goes to my neck as he grabs it, but he's gentle about it, which is not what I was expecting. My heated neck sizzles at his cool touch. "Rules are not meant to be broken, Claire."

"I won't do it ever again. I promise. I'm sorry." Alex lets go of me and steps back, the anger slowly fading from him.

Alex glowers at me before turning and heading back to his room. I hear him talk to the women. I'm too ashamed and aroused, to move. My legs are shaking slightly. 'What do I do now? Does he want me to leave? Did I ruin everything?' A door in Alex's room opens and closes.

'Did he leave? With the women?'

"Claire, come in here." My heart lurches at the sound of him saying my name. I enter his bedroom again, this time with permission. "Yes, Alex?" I look around the room and see that Alex has removed the blood- soaked bedspread from his bed. "Sit down." 'Is he still mad at me?' "Please."

I walk to the other side of Alex's room, over to his bed, and take a seat at the edge of it, no remnants of blood are seen, except on Alex. Alex walks over to the bed and sits next to me.

Alex starts unbuttoning his blood- stained shirt. I can't help but gaze at him as he does. "I am sorry you have to see me like this."

'I'm not, Nice abs, His body is so amazing...' He takes off his shirt and uses it to clean up his face and hands. Then he tosses it on the ground next to the bedspread. Alex understands that my silence means something. He concludes that I am being afraid of him. "She's going to be fine, just so you know. "

"I believe you. Um, who was she?" 'I hope I don't sound like a jealous girlfriend!'

"She's.... no one you need to concern yourself with. Just a simple human."

"I'm not concerned. Is she a girlfriend of your?" Alex lowers his eyebrows and stares at me.

'Oh, great. He's going to get mad at me again and tell me to mind my own business.'

"No. She's not." I'm relieved, but then I feel guilty. 'James...'

"It seemed like she enjoyed it." 'Did he lure her here, somehow, with his powers? Was he able to hypnotize her? If he has hypnotizing powers that would explain why I have been feeling so strongly for him!'

"You have to understand Claire, She came to me on her own. She.... she wanted that to happen."

"So you can't hypnotize people?"

"Not really. Of course, people are naturally drawn to vampires because of their attractiveness, so that might be a little...hypnotic. But I didn't trick her into thinking it felt good."

"Is she... a regular visitor?"

"I didn't want you to find out... like this. I was going to tell you, but I wanted to wait for a better time." Alex moves closer to me. "That women you saw sis bonded to me."

"What does that mean?"

"She drank my blood. I drank hers. So now she is completely and utterly mine. She begs for me."

'I know I should be repulsed by this. I should want to run far away from this dangerous, beautiful man and never look back. But why don't I want to? Why do I feel even more drawn to him?' I have almost completely forgotten about James' existence now. My mind is so occupied with thoughts as I try and process all of the information that Alex has just told me.

"I'm sorry, Claire." He moves away from me, towards his bedroom window as his shoulders sag. I realize he's sad. I move closer to him in the middle of the room.

"I'm not afraid of you, Alex." Alex leans his fist against the frame of the window. He doesn't speak. "Alex, please." The sound of me begging seems to be enough to get him to turn around and look at me. He looks disappointed in himself. "Look at everything you've done for me, and the things you're still doing. I trust you...." Alex approaches me. He doesn't use his super-speed this time. His steps are slow and hopeful.

'He's so beautiful it hurts.' I take both of Alex's hands in mine and stand close to him, gazing up into his eyes. Then I give him a smouldering smirk and lean into his ear to whisper to him. "I want you make me feel like she did." Alex's body tightens when my breath tickles his ear.

His hands let go of me and grip my waist, instead. I look back at him. His eyes are full of fire. 'I wish I knew what he was thinking.'

I throw my arms around Alex's neck. Then my lips crash onto his. Alex reacts by moving one hand to clutch my lower back and tangles the other in my hair. All of my senses are invaded by him, He tastes faintly metallic, yet sweet.

His gentle hair- tugging and body- grabbing are enough to drive me completely wild. I feel as if I could drown myself in his earthy, manly scent.

"You have no idea what you do to me." I feel myself gliding weightlessly through the air, in his arms.

The next thing I know, Alex is grabbing my hips and setting me on top of his dresser. His tongue enters my mouth and dances around hungrily. I moan with intense pleasure. 'I can't believe he can make me feel this good.'

Alex spreads my legs and presses himself against me. His lips leave my mouth and move to my neck. I moan as he nibbles on my neck gently, but not enough to pierce my skin.

I claw at his back, my entire body buzzing from how badly I want him. "I don't want to hurt you."

"I want you to."

Alex speaks into my neck. Feeling him makes me want to scream out. 'How am I capable to feel all of this? Impossible.'

The two of us are breathing heavily. Then suddenly, he pulls away from me and steps back, removing my hands from himself and panting. "Claire..." I hop off the dresser, still yearning for his touch.

Alex clears his throat. "It's late. We have a big day tomorrow. You should get some sleep.

I try my hardest not to let him see my pout. "I suppose you're right."

***

I'm back in my room, sitting on the edge of my bed. "What am I doing?" 'Now that I have had a chance to calm down and get some distance from Alex. I realize how terrible that was of me, James is still in the picture. I know it was wrong, but I can't help myself when I am around Alex. I think there must be something magical about this world that is making me feel this way.' I stand up, unable to sit still.

'It's like all of my senses are heightened here. I have never felt this way before.' I walk over to my wardrobe. "I guess I'll get changed for bed." 'I don't want to look too tempting. I'm still not tired yet! I need a distraction or something to help me sleep.'

I leave my room and explore the castle, checking out various rooms and hallways. I see a beautiful ballroom, a masculine, dark study, other guest rooms, and even a lush greenhouse. 'This castle is straight out of a fairy-tale!'

I got to know more about the different creatures on this land. Just as they were earlier, they are excited to talk to me, and even more excited that I want to learn about them. 'Wow! Fairies, Manticores, and even real gnomes working in the greenhouse! I can't believe they all actually exist!'

I stop walking when I reach a pair of giant, wooden double doors. I go to open them, but turn my head and Alex walking down the hall towards me. "There you are."

His face looks relieved. My breath catches in my throat at the sight of him. "Hey."

"I knocked on your door, but you weren't in there. I wondered if you had..."

'Wait, was he worried that I changed my mind about being afraid of him and decided to leave?'

"I've heard you've been making lots of friends around the castle."

"I have! Everyone is so incredible, Alex! I feel like I am in a dream!"

"Well, since you're awake, I was wondering if you would like to talk to me."

"I thought we were supposed to be sleeping."

"Yeah, well... I can't." I swoon as excitement rises inside of me. "Me neither."

"Where would you like to go? We can go anywhere in the castle! You pick."

"Anywhere?" There is a twinkle in his eye as he nods his head. "Yes, Anywhere."

"There's still plenty of tea left. Shall we go to the dining room?" Alex looks slightly disappointed, but then he smiles and nods his head.

In the dining room, he sits at the head of the table. I seat adjacent to him. The maid sees us two and grabs fresh tea and new cups. "So, you've learned a bit about my world. Tell me a little more about yours."

I and Alex spends hours talking and laughing and getting to know each other. I finish my tea and go back to the bedroom together. Alex takes some of my hair and tucks it behind my ear. I lean my cheek into the palm of his hand. Alex strokes my soft ski briefly, then let's go of me as his face turns serious. "I want to apologize again for what happened earlier."

"Alex, really it's okay."

"No, it's not. But I promise- It will not ever happen again. I just..."

"What?"

"I don't know why I can't seem to control myself when I am around you." I touch his hand timidly and feel sparks fly. "I feel the same way." I and Alex talk some more until I feel myself getting super sleepy and having trouble keeping my eyes open. "We should get you in bed."

I snap my eyes open. "No, I'm fine. I promise"

"I just saw you doze off."

"No, I didn't!" I and Alex playfully argue back and forth. Alex gets to his feet and holds out his hand to me. "Claire, come on. I'm insisting you go to sleep."

"Make me."

Alex's eyes fill with desire. He springs, picking me up as if I weigh close to nothing. I wrap my legs around him and giggle. He stands there holding me close to him. His smouldering face is so sexy that I feel myself becoming aroused again. "Don't test me, Claire."

Chapter 6

I wake up refreshed the next morning. 'Finally, a good night's rest!' I get ready for the day and leave my room to head to breakfast.

I turn and close the bedroom door behind. When I start walking down the hall, my body slams into a tall, handsome, brooding man. 'Wait, that's not a man. That's a vampire!'

I notice that the vampires doesn't dress like the other workers in the castle. I want to appear brave and unafraid of him. "Can I help you? Who are you and what are you doing here?" The vampire looks at me up and down, his eyes narrowing as if he's trying to read me.

"I can ask you the same question, Miss! What do you think you're doing? A human! Wandering around a Lord Eden castle!" I'm about to answer him when he takes my elbow. A feeling shoots up my arm that I can't quite explain. It's almost as if the vampire is made of electricity. I realize he must have felt the same sensation because we both freeze and look at each other at the same time.

His eyes soften, but only for a moment, then he goes back to being angry. "Come." The man starts pulling me down the hallway.

I try yanking my arm out of the man's grasp. "Let me go! I'm not going anywhere with you!" The vampire only tightens his grip. "Oh, is that so?" I feel the same angry vampire's eyes on me again. 'Is he... checking me out?' "Look, I'm sorry. I don't mean any trouble. Really. Please, just let me go." The vampire chuckles darkly. "Absolutely not!"

Fear builds inside of me, all the way to my core when I realize that the vampire holding tightly onto me isn't going to let me go. "Alex!" Alex's bedroom door flies open and he races into the hall, his eyes are full of rage as he bears his fangs, ready to protect me. "Alex, tell him to let me go!"

Alex looks at me and the hand gripping my arm. He relaxes as he sees the vampire holding me. "Let her go."

"Surely this human can't mean much to you."

"That's none of your business. Let her go. NOW!"

The two go back and forth, throwing insults at each other until the vampire finally let's go of me. "You know she doesn't belong here."

"It's my castle, so I shall do as I please."

"It's not right!"

"Stop holding on to the past."

"Stop trying to fix things that were never broken. Traditions are traditions for a reason."

"Times are changing. You need to accept that."

"Not when it comes to vampires and humans."

'I need to say something, why should I hear them bicker.'

"She can't be here. It's unacceptable. I can't believe-"

"Stop talking about me like I'm not standing here, I have a name, it's Claire." Both the vampires turn and look at me. Alex shakes his head and sighs. "Don't interrupt me again, Claire."

They go back and forth a couple more times before the angry vampire stops talking and shakes his head. "I am not going to stand here and fight with you any longer, Alex. It's not worth it."

"Exactly." The vampire turns to me and glares one last time before storming off.

"What the hell was that all about?" Alex takes my hand and gives me a gentle smile. "Nothing you'll have to worry about again, I assure you." He slowly pulls me back toward my bedroom. I stare down the hallway after the man. He is no longer there. A light bulb flickers on in my brain. "Alex, who was that?" Alex grimaces and stare in the same direction I am, his jaw clenched.

"That, unfortunately was my brother, Jack!"

'Oh my god! His brother?'

Chapter 7

I am standing alone at the terrace, when I felt a figure standing behind me.

"Jack!"
Dark clouds appear overhead along with thunder and lightning. Jack uses his super speed to appear right next to me. He grips my arm tightly, and the same electric feeling surges through me again.

"You're going to come with me this time."

Jack pulls me to a part of the castle that I have seen before. "Sit. I'm tying you up." I sit on a single chair in a dark, musty room. Jack uses tightly knotted ropes to restrain me. I find myself wearing nothing but lingerie. 'When did I change into this outfit?'

I look back at Jack and notice that the corners of his mouth are covered in blood. "Oh my god!"

"I've just finished feeding. But I still feel so..... Thirsty." Jack breathes in my ear, sending shivers down my spine. "You should fear me, Claire."

"I'm not afraid of you, Jack." Jack growls and reaches down and entangles his hand in my hair, his eyes gazing longingly at my plump lips. I let out a small moan when he tugs on my hair.

"So you want me to feed on you, then?"

I am powerless to stop him. 'It feels so fucking good.' "Jack! Please.... feed on...-me...."

"Jack! Please-- feed on -me... "The room become weirdly silent.

"Jack?" Lightning flashes through the tiniest window illuminating Jack. His fang are out and he's lunging at me, about to attack.

"Help me!" The lightning disappears and suddenly, he's gone again.

"Is anyone there?" Lightning illuminates again, and this time, Jack is straddling me as his hands are roaming all over my body. "Jack!" I'm unable to do anything but sit in the chair and let him have his way with me.

Jack trails his hand down my neck. I gasp... Thunder booms and lightning shines into the room. Jack isn't touching me anymore. His mouth is dripping blood again, as he yanks hard on my hair to expose my throat. "Please don't kill me!"

That's when my eyes snap open. I'm back in my bedroom in Alex's castle. I had only been dreaming again. That's when I hear the maid knock on my door. "Come in!"

"Good morning! You look tired, did you not sleep well? "

"Oh! Um, I'm fine, thank you." I am tired, though, I'd been tossing and turning all night having dreams about Jack.

'I don't think I should tell the maid about what's bothering me.
'

"Good! Then up, up, up! Alex has quite the day planned, and we have to make sure you are looking your absolute best! "

I get up and go over to my wardrobe with the maid, who wants to help me pick out my outfit.

I let the maid help me get dressed and ready for my day. "Do you think Jack is going to be in the town today as well?"

"Doubtful. He likes it up in his castle."

"Has he and Alex ever gotten along."

"If they did, it was a long long time ago."

"Have you talked to Alex yet today?"

"Yes, he is downstairs having breakfast…"

"How does he seem?"

"He's a little stressed out. Days like these are very important to him, you know."

"Of course. I'll be happy to do whatever he needs. I hope he wins. "

"Me too, dear. Me too."

"But I am slightly nervous about having another run in with Jack."

The maid goes to reply, but before she does, Alex walks into my bedroom. He is well dressed and his hair is neatly styled. He looks tense.

'I hope he didn't overhear me talking about Jack' "good morning, Alex!"

"Are you ready to go?"

"Yes... "My stomach dips at his mood. Maybe he's just stressed, or maybe he did hear me talking about his brother.

We both walk down the stairs and head out of the gigantic door as I spot a magnificent horse-drawn carriage. "This is beautiful!" A worker opens the door to the carriage and reveals royal purple tufted seating inside.

Alex gets inside first. The worker takes my hand and helps me inside the carriage. I step inside the carriage and take a seat across from Alex. 'It will be easier to behave myself if I'm not touching him, and I am still worried he might be upset with me.'

"You look beautiful, Claire. Are you excited?"

"I can't wait." I and Alex ride into town and make conversation about what to expect for the day. It's going to be a long ride and we have the carriage to ourselves. "I know Jack doesn't approve of anything I am wanting to change, but I don't care."

"You don't?"

"My family has always been so traditional. I might be the only one who wants to see the change, but if that's the case, then so be it. I know I can make Night City a better Place. Humans shouldn't have to live in the bad part of town and be afraid to leave their homes at night. I'm tired of the segregation. It's not right."

"Are humans usually afraid of vampires?"

"Because of our history, yes. They see us as killers, even if we don't do that anymore. Every time someone goes missing, the town assumes it was a vampire's doing."

"But you don't think that's true?"

"I don't." After his response, the carriage is filled with silence. I'm not able to shake off the thoughts and questions about the other night.

"Alex, tell me what it feels like to be fed on." Alex's eyes darken and fill with hunger. I see him Glance at my neck. "You really want to know?"

"Mhnn."

"It feels like the best sex of your life. There is no other better feeling in the world for you humans."

"I wish you would show me."

"I don't want to harm you, Claire." I stare at him seductively and put my hand on his thigh, slowly moving it upwards. "You don't have to feed on me. I can think of other things."

Chapter 8

Alex licks his lips and reaches for my waist gently pulling me on top of him. His hands are low on my back, clutching onto me desperately.
Alex goes to kiss me, but I dive into his neck and suck on his delicious skin making him groan with pleasure. "Claire." He pushes me off of him and onto the seat across from him. I'm stunned for a moment but that's when he gets up and sits beside me clutching my upper thigh underneath my dress and making me gasp.

We two kiss again as I move closer to him, wanting him to touch me even deeper as I start throbbing for him. As if he can read my mind, Alex trails his hands down my stomach and I feel his fingers stroke over the soft material of my unders. "Alex!"

Alex stares at me with a longing gaze. I arch my back, my body begging for more. Alex notices my desperation and moves my panties to the side and starts massaging me with his fingers. I lean back in my seat and moan.

At the sound of it, Alex instinctively reaches out and grabs a fistful of my hair with his free hand. The sensation makes my body tremble in ecstasy. "Fuck..."

"You are so wet, Claire." He pushes one finger inside of me and I claw at the purple velvet seats. 'It feels so amazing!' Alex takes his finger out and massages my sex in slow, small circles, gradually moving faster and faster as I moan loudly and cling onto his neck.

My head tilted back as my eyes stay closed.

"Do you want me to stop?"

"Please...No..." He inserts two fingers into me this time, and I scratch at his back, losing myself. He moves faster, his fingers going deeper, hitting me in just the right spot.

I am unable to breathe as the pleasure grows more and more intense inside of me. "Oh god, Alex! Just like that!" Hearing how aroused I am, Alex moans and nibbles on my ear. I Begin to climax. My mouth opens and I press my pelvis into Alex's hand as hard as I can as he keeps the steady rhythm of moving in and out of me.

I'm so aroused that moans keep escaping me, making Alex groan loudly. "Alex, I'm going to..." Every muscle in my body tenses and loosens at the same time.

I cry out loud and forget everything around me except for how good I feel. My thighs clench tightly around Alex's hand as I finish, as he slowly takes it out, my body's so sensitive that it feels like he's electrocuting me. "That was amazing."

Alex kiss me tenderly.

***

I and Alex ride the rest of the way to town in each other's arms. When the carriage stops, I get out to walk around the city on foot. "Well, Claire. What would you like to see first?"

"I'm curious to see where the humans live." Alex nods and lets the guards lead us to a shabby part of town. The humans are outside their homes, cleaning. Shopping, and chatting with one another.

"Hello Benjamin!" I and Alex stop by a busy market stall and talk to an old man who seems quite taken with Alex. As I talk to more humans, I realize that they all seem to like him.

"Wow, Alex. With their votes, I really think you could win this!"

"With you by my side, I think I could too."

I and Alex take a seat on a bench by the city fountain. "I knew having you here would help." I feel proud of him and grateful that he chose me to be on his arm all day. "Alex, you didn't need me. They liked you all on your own!"

"But them seeing me around town escorting a human helped make them feel more comfortable around me." I lean my head on his shoulder. "I really am grateful for you." I smile at him and realize just how much I like being here.

***

Back at the castle, I'm about to head to bed. I and Alex stand outside my room to talk about today. "Are you okay if we do that again tomorrow?"

"I'd love it."

"Good. Get some sleep. I'll be up late doing some research on how to get you home, as promised." I want to tell him that there's no rush to get back, but he talks again before I can. "What do you want to do tomorrow?"

"Let's go back to the city square."

***

The next day in town, I and Alex sit by the fountain again and talk to creatures. I spend the whole day with everyone, and I'm so tired, I nearly fall asleep in Alex's arms in the carriage ride home.

At night when I and Alex head back to Night city, I take part in a Parade and ride on afloat. "Just smile and wave." I do as I'm told, and when I scan the crowd of people, I gasp.

Jack is standing in the opening of an alleyway, his eyes watching me with intense curiosity. "Are you alright?" I go back to smiling and waving at everyone. "Of course!"

When the float ends, Alex is pulled into a conversation, so I decide to take a look at the area where I saw Jack. When I reach the alleyway, Jack is no longer there. 'Did I really see him? Ugh I have to snap out of it!' I hate to admit it, but I have been thinking about Jack a lot since we two met.

More days pass as I and Alex ride into town, meeting people and making speeches. I'm becoming used to this lifestyle. 'I've barely even thought about James.' When the weekends arrive and I get back to the castle, Alex takes me in his arms and swings me around. "What would I do without you?"

"I am so proud of you, Alex." He beams at me and give me passionate kiss.

I'm sitting at the breakfast table with Alex, enjoying a quiet weekend morning. "How is it?"

"It's wonderful, as usual." Alex takes my hand and holds it on top of the table. He strokes my skin softly with his thumb as he gazes deeply into my eyes. "I wanted to ask you something."

"And what might that be?"

"There is a ball coming up. I think you'd love it. Would you like to go with me?"

"Are you kidding me? That sounds incredible!" I grin excitedly and lean across the table to kiss Alex on the cheek. "It's settled then! Why don't you head into town and pick out a dress? Get anything you want. My treat. But don't stay out after dark. It gets dangerous for humans then."

"Got it. I'll leave now, so I can be back soon." Alex flashes me a genuine smile as I leave for the town ride by myself.

The coachman drops me off in the human part of the city, where the shops that Alex recommended are.

I say hello to familiar faces and browse around until I finally find a shop with all the best options. 'These dresses are stunning! I have to try them all on!' I head into a changing room and try on dress after dress, trying to decide on the best one.

"Do you need any help?" I turn and see a gorgeous women standing behind me. "I'm Dawn, work here."

"Oh, hello!"

"Here, let me tie that for you." I and Dawn make pleasant conversation as she helps me with the dresses. I tell Dawn all about my world and how I got here. 'It's so nice to have found a human my age that I could talk to. I feel as if I have made a new friend.'

"Do you miss it back home, then?"

"Yes, I do. But I am also having a good time here, so I am not in hurry to go back!"

"So you're enjoying all this time you're spending with Alex? A vampire?"

"Alex is wonderful and very hospitable. I love it here."

"Have you met his brother, Jack?"

"Yes. He seems scary, but if he's Alex's brother then I'm sure there's some good in him, too."

"But you don't really know them yet."

"What's that supposed to mean?"

"I am just saying, don't trust them so blindly. They are all vampires, after all."

"How do you know so much about them? I would love to learn more as well."

"The Eldon family has a lot of dark secrets. Alex puts up a front so that no one ever finds him out. James might seem scary, but at least he doesn't try to hide who he really is."

"I guess so! I actually do have a hard time figuring out what Alex is thinking about sometimes. I appreciate you telling me. I'll be careful." I find the perfect dress, thanks to Dawn, she wraps it up for me and bills it to the castle.

"It was wonderful to meet you, Dawn!"

"Wait! I am having so much fun talking with you. Would you like to come to my house for dinner? See the real way humans live around here?"

I am happy to have made a friend, but Alex told me not to stay out after dark. "That sounds lovely, Dawn. I wish I could, but Alex is requesting me back at his castle this evening."

"Have the coachman tell him you're staying at a friend's!"

"I'm really, sorry Dawn. I did enjoy talking with you."

"Do you not care about my warning? I really think you'd be better off coming to my house than to Alex's castle."

"I promise you, Alex won't hurt me."

"You don't know that, you hardly know him! Just come on."

"Maybe we can meet tomorrow instead? Are you available? I'd love for you to come and see the castle!"

"Absolutely not. I'm not going there. And you shouldn't, either. I am just looking out for you and trying to be a good friend."

"I appreciate that."

"And it's just so rare that I get to meet new people. It can be incredibly lonely here." I begin to feel uncomfortable at her not taking no for an answer. I know Alex wouldn't like it if I didn't return to the castle, and I don't want to worry him. "I'm sorry, I have to go."

I turn and start walking out of the shop, but that's when Dawn calls out to me. "Claire, wait! You dropped this!" I turn back around, and instead of handing me something, Dawn blows a powder in my face.

I cough and sputter trying to close my stinging eyes. "What did you do?" Dawn grabs my wrist and pulls me inside the shop. Then she closes and locks the door as well as shuts all the windows. "Why are you doing this?" I fall to the ground. The last thing I remember before everything goes black is Dawn tying my hands together. 'Someone please help me....'

***

I wake up groggy and confused with no idea where I am and how I got there. My hands are tied behind a chair. My neck feels sore because of being unconscious for long hours, the exhaustion is catching up on me. 'How long have I been here?' "Hello? Somebody help me! Please!" Dawn reaches out quickly and throws open the door of my room giving me a look of exasperation.

"Will you shut up?!" She is furious and confused as she approaches me. I try to break free from the ropes, but I am not strong enough. "Why would I untie you? Now stop yelling!"

"Let me go, Dawn!"

"Not a chance." Dawn paces around the room with her hands behind her back, angrily kicking random things. "I don't understand!-"

"Let me go!"

"The powder should have kept you unconscious much longer than this! How are you awake?"

"Alex must be looking around for me! And when he finds out you did this to me, he's going to be furious."

"You really think he's going to come save you?" I struggle against the ties some more even though it proves to be useless.

"Look, I don't know who you are, but I promise you, Alex is going to be really mad if you don't release me right this instant!" Dawn laughs maniacally. 'My threats seem to mean nothing to her!'

"No keep quite or I'll have to make you..." Dawn gives me a last look of anger and frantically leaves the room. 'I don't think I am going to find a way out of this. How long is she going to keep me in here?' A commotion sounds outside of the room. I hear banging and muffled noises, then suddenly Jack busts into the room. "Jack?"

Chapter 9

I aren't sure whether to be scared or relieved to see him. I'm confused to see him, standing before me. Dawn is nowhere to be seen. "What are you doing here?" Jack races towards me with impatience. "Are you hurt?"

"Where is Dawn?"

"Don't worry about her." Jack rips the ropes off of me with ease pulling me out of the chair and into his warm body. I fall weak in relief, my limbs barely able to move as I let him hold me. "We need to get you out of here." I feel so overcome with emotion not knowing what to think. Everything is too overwhelming for me, it's hard to trust anyone.

"I'm so tired."

"I'm going to carry you then, okay?" I shake my head at Jack's question and begin standing up be myself. "I think I can walk." I take a couple of steps and stumble but Jack is quick to grab my arm so I don't fall over. "Are you sure you're okay?" "Yes, I'm fine. Let's just go, before she comes back!"

I and Jack leave the place I was locked up in and step outside into the woods. I had been trapped in a small cottage right in the middle of the forest! "How did we get here? It's not safe in the forest!"

I move away for Jack and try to sprint my way out of the forest still unsure of which way to go. All I know is that the forest is dangerous to be in at night. 'And I don't know if I can trust Jack to protect me!' Jack catches up with ease.

"Are you crazy? You can't be out here alone! Let me help you, Claire."

"I don't want to be in here anymore! What if she comes back and uses something against me again? She said it was supposed to keep me unconscious for a long time." I and Jack head out of the forest. Now that I have escaped the cottage and feel a little more awake, a million things are concerning me, and every noise I hear is making me jumpy. "Jack, who is Dawn? Why did she do that to me? She doesn't even know me!"

"She feels threatened by you."

"Threatened? Why?"

"It's hard to explain." I and Jack stand and face each other. "I want answers, Jack." Jack nods sternly. "There is something you need to know about Dawn and Alex."

'I don't see how either of them could possibly have anything in common!' "Go on."

"You see... Dawn is Alex's ex- lover, Claire. That is something he should have told you." My heart falls to my feet. I am disappointed to know Alex has been romantic with other humans before. But I'm aware that his past choices don't define him. "Ah... what does that have to do with me, then? Is she Jealous?"

Jack doesn't answer right away leaving me bewildered. "No, it's not that. Dawn thinks you are the key to winning the election. She doesn't want that to happen." My facial expressions drop as soon as I hear that, confusion spreads all over my face.

"Me? How could I possibly be the key? That makes no sense. Yeah right."

"Um, there's more."

"What?"

"She also thinks you are going to unleash an almighty power that has been lost for many, many years."

'This makes no sense, what is Jack trying to say? I'm not even from their land and yet they're scared of me?' I start walking away from Jack.

"Claire, where are you going?"

"To get some real answers."

Jack catches me just in time and flips me over making me face him. He lifts my chin up his fore-finger as his gaze fixated on me. "I am telling you the truth, Claire." Fear courses through, yet something in me tells me to believe him. "Dawn doesn't want Alex to be in charge, and she will do whatever she has to in order to make sure that power is not brought back to Night City.."

"I don't know what she thinks I'm going to do. I'm scared she will do something like this again."

"I know. It was a good thing I found you in the cottage." I give Jack a genuine smile and surprisingly he smiles back at me. "Well

I have no idea what I am supposed to do now." I feel so confused, scared and tired. I just want to lie down. "Try not to worry too much about it now. You need to rest."

"I just don't get it, Jack. I am only human. How can any of this be happening?" Jack grabs me by the elbow, similarly to how he did back at the castle. He gives me a very serious look.

"Just know this, Claire. Alex is selfish and power- hungry. You need to stay away from him."

"That can't be true."

"But yet, it is. My brother only cares about himself."

"But he's been so nice to me since I got here. Tell me what exactly makes you feel this way about him?"

"It's been this way for over a lifetime! He's always wanted to make all the rules and important decisions. He's always climbed over anyone and everyone to make his way to the top."

"If he's as selfish as you suggest, why did he agree to help me find a way back to my world?"

"Do you really think he's been trying to help you?"

'Alex has told me he's been working on a way to get me back home. He wouldn't lie to me, right?' "I don't know Jack…"

"Believe me. I don't have anything to gain by telling you this information." Jack resumes walking at a normal human speed. "Come, Claire. We shouldn't linger in these woods any longer." I remember the day I came to this world when Alex had been mauled by the Ogre.

'Alex was nearly unconscious! If another Ogre comes through here, will Jack protect me?' A growl sounds in the far, far distance.

I jump and continue along my way with Jack. "Where are you taking me then? Since you don't want me to go back to Alex's castle.

"My home is close by. You'll be staying there for the night." I feel a tingling sensation inside of me that I can't quite place. "Oh am I? Do I not get any other options?" Jack looks back at me over his shoulder with a playful smirk on his face. "I mean it Claire. You don't know this town like I do. My castle is the best option if you want to stay safe and away from Dawn."

I shudder at the mere mention of Dawn. "Fine. I will come to your castle. Only if you promise not to harm me in any way!" I stand behind him and wait. Jack turns back to me, looking tired.

"I promise, Claire." I and Jack take a shortcut, and when I break through the trees, I find myself in front of the gates to Jack's castle. 'It still looks creepy to me.' Jack eyes me with a curious expression as he unlocks the gate and lets me through.

When I get inside, I discover that while the castle may have looked intimidating and unsetting on the outside, it's actually gorgeous, cozy and intimate on the inside. 'I was not expecting this! It's beautiful in here! And wow, the artwork.' I step closer to a landscape painting of a beautiful yellow meadow. There are a lot more painting like this through the castle.

I purse my lips as Jack holds out his arm. "Let me take you to your room. I'm sure you want to freshen up and get out of those clothes." I take his arm and Jack leads me into an incredibly luxurious, dark colored bedroom. "Does this work for you?"

I gasp at the beauty of it. "I'll take that as a yes."

Jack shuts the door and I head over to pick out an outfit from the wardrobe. I finish freshening up and then head to bed.

In the back of my mind, I'm still thinking about Alex. I'm wondering why Alex hasn't come looking for me, and if all the things Jack had to say about him are true.

I let out a heavy sigh, and drift off to sleep.

***

I wake up the next morning in Jack's guest room. 'Ugh, why do I feel like I barely got any sleep last night?' I kept tossing and turning all night long because of having nightmares about Dawn.

I get out of bed and freshen up. 'It feels so different, but I haven't got much time to waste.' I leave my room and walk down the hallway of the castle to look for Jack.

"Jack?" I get no response 'Maybe I should let him know I'm leaving with a note or something? I don't think we're close enough for me to do that.'

I leave the castle without finding Jack.

'It's probably a good thing that I head back anyway. I need to talk to Alex about Dawn and what I learned yesterday.' I start making my way back to Alex's Castle feeling slightly uneasy and afraid. I don't know what is about to happen.

When I finally arrive at Alex's Castle, I quietly step inside. The first thing I hear is Alex yelling frantically. He appears to be talking to a castle worker. "You're sure you haven't seen her? She wasn't in her room? Her bed hadn't been slept in? Nobody saw her come home?"

'Oh, my goodness, is Alex actually worried about me after all? Had he been looking for me all night?

"Alex?" He doesn't reply. "Alex! I'm here!" I go upstairs and turn corner after corner.

My stomach is dancing nervously as I hear Alex's footsteps approaching me. "Claire? Is that really you?" Alex's eyes are full of relief when he sees me standing before him. "Oh, thank god." Alex races towards me pulling me into his embrace instantly. He gives me a passionate kiss.

The kiss makes me forget things for an instant, I just want to melt into him and savor this beautiful moment. But I'm reminded of all the worries and confusion. 'Was he actually worried about m, or was he just missing his good luck charm?'

"What happened?"

"I was on the human side of town shopping for dresses like you suggested yesterday."

"Why didn't you come back?"

"A women named Dawn-"Alex's face instantly drops as he hears Dawn's name, I take a deep breath and continue telling him what happened. "She kidnapped me and took me to a cottage in the middle of the woods."

"My god!"

"She knocked me out with a mysterious powder. It was Jack who come to rescue me. He told me about Dawn and why she did that to me."

"Claire, I assure you nothing like this will ever happen again. Are you alright?"

"I don't know, Alex. It was really scary." I look at Alex and take a deep breath before bringing up the things Jack told me. "Jack seems to think that you don't actually care about me or that you really want to help me get home." Alex seems to be getting tensed as his neck vein starts popping, it scares me but I gulp down my fear and wait for his answer.

"Jack is lying. The entire time you were shopping I was working here, trying to help you find a way home. I might have found a solution, too! But I'm not sure how dangerous it will be."

"Alex, tell me more about me being the key. What was Jack talking about?"

"Well... You are very helpful when it comes to touring the city and talking to the townspeople. They all really like you, and I do think it is helping my chances. I wouldn't want to keep it from you, but it's not like I'm just using you to win the election Claire."

"Is that it?"

"Dawn is dangerous. I will do whatever it takes to keep her away from you." I aren't satisfied with Alex's answers but he did give me some information. My belief in the two brothers is at equivalence.

"So I am the key which is important for you?" I could notice the shift in Alex's mood as if he knows what I'm thinking. "Claire I'm not sure what Dawn knows and I don't, but you do have an effect on these people." Alex takes a few steps towards me, his hands reaching out for my face, cupping it. His piercing gaze turns soft while looking at me. "You make me see the best in all. Humans aren't very used to kindness when it comes to Vampires." Alex reaches out for my shoulders and gently places his hands on them.

Chapter 10

"I promise Claire, I'll never let you get hurt again. I have a lot of things to do today since the ball is approaching."

"Hm, right, that's today."

"As a Lord Eden guest, it is very important that you look your best, the maid will help you out with the outfit."

"Uh okay…"

"Everyone's going to be there, I know you will impress them. All of them are from the most powerful and influential families around."

"Whatever you need."

He gives me a kind smile. 'Alex's Ball is important but he doesn't seem to care about me at all. Was Jack right?' My mind fills up with confusion again, but I try not to think about it.

"Thank you, Claire. It's going to be a wonderful night."

I feel like snapping at him, but I gulp down my anger. I have to be polite because he has done a lot for me. "Thank you Alex. I am looking forward to it." I leave the study quickly as tears start forming in my eyes.

Part of me thinks, if I want to get myself back home, I am going to have to figure it out all on my own. I think of all the possibilities and about all the conversations I've had with people to find that one answer.

I distinctly remember the big double doors I was going to check out earlier before Alex stopped me a couple of days ago. I head through the castle, trying to remember where I saw the place. It seems like a lifetime goes by before I finally recognize the two massive towering double doors. 'I hope there is something useful in here.'

I open the doors and find myself inside a gigantic, beautiful library. "Oh my gosh!" I feel like I could faint from how amazing it all seems to be. Deep inside I know there has to be information on how to get home. 'I can spend hours in here.'

I open lots of books and skim through shelves learning a ton of interesting facts about this world and others. The supply of knowledge is endless.

'As fun as this is, I still need to figure out how to get home. None of this has helped me yet.' I look around for some more places in the library that I haven't searched yet. I spot a tiny spiral staircase leading to a row of bookshelves with pretty painted spines. On the other side of the library is a small door between some shelves that I haven't explored yet.

I walk towards the door and turn the handle. To my amazing surprise, it is unlocked. 'This is a good sign!' I enter the room and find myself in a dusty, dark place.

It seems like this is where one would put books that hey either want to get rid of or don't want other people finding. "What is that?" At the far end of the room, there is a glass case. I approach it. Inside, there is a book with a cover threaded in gold, very similar to the one I found at my house. 'What is this doing here? Why do I feel so compelled to open it?'

I brush my fingers along the cover of the book whilst picking it up. I know there must be something important inside. I am mesmerized and enthralled to find out.

They are even more powerful than the Lord Eden family. "This is so interesting!" As I continue to read. I suddenly recognize the similarities in the book. Feels likes I've heard this story before. Maybe from a story book when I was a child. 'It seems so familiar!'

My eyes go wide as I learn about a princess, I skim through the pages, and to my surprise, and the story seems to have the answers I'm looking for. 'A lost vampire princess!'

***

Back in my room, the maid has assembled a team of workers and stylists to help me do my hair and makeup and get dressed for the ball.

I'm upset that I didn't find the information I was looking for about how to get myself home, but soon the nervousness for the ball takes over me.

The maid can sense something is wrong. "What's wrong dear?"

"Oh, it's nothing."

"It doesn't look like nothing."

"I promise, I'm fine. Maybe just a little tired. I didn't sleep very well last night."

"That's probably because you didn't sleep in your cozy bed here!"

"Maybe." The maid pats me on the head. "You really need to cheer up, Claire! It's not every day you get to go to a ball! Especially as a Lord Eden Guest. Not to mention a Human Guest."

I flash a genuine smile at the maid and proceed to get ready. I find myself getting happier and more excited about the evening as the maid and the rest of the workers help me get ready. There is so much extravaganza, frills, and pretty colors. It's almost as if I'm in a fairy tale.

As I sit in a chair and let my hair get worked on, the maid strikes up a conversation with me again. "What are you most excited for tonight, Claire?"

"I'm curious to see the powerful families Alex was talking about. Are all of them vampires?"

"Not all of them! But you will be meeting a lot interesting people tonight. And some of them are eager to meet you, as well."

"Really?!" 'I wonder why that could be.' After my hair and makeup are finally complete, it is time to get changed for the ball. "I wish I could buy the dress from yesterday's shop." I sigh in disappointment because after I were taken by Dawn, I have no idea what happened to my dress. It would've looked gorgeous on me.

"Well there are plenty of options for you here!" The maid goes and rummages around in the wardrobe. "I think these two are the perfect options!"

As I look at myself in the mirror, my reflection amazes me. The attire really suits me and the feeling of confidence washes over. 'This doesn't even look like me!' My mind fills up with memories of my first day in this magical town. 'Home seems like a distant memory now. Being here feels more normal than being back there.' I start missing my world less every day, this town has a different vibe to it which is unexplained.

I take a deep breath and start off the night assertively.

***

When I enter the gorgeous ballroom, I can't help but stop and stare at everything. There is a charming string quartet playing beautiful music in the corner and a beautiful dance floor with expertly twirling pairs dancing about. Everyone is dressed in expensive pretty clothes. 'I have never seen anything like this.'

On one side of the room, I notice Alex, his shiny black lapelled regency tux makes him look even more dashing, and his eyes instantly meet mine as he gives me a warm smile. I look at his eyes light up. I can tell he wants me to go over to him. On other side of the room, I also spot Jack. He looks equally happy to see me too, He looks over at me as we two make intense eye contact.

Jack's hair is styled differently and his attire compliments his dark brooding personality. He beckons me over to him. 'What should I do?'

I smile at Alex and give Jack an apologetic wave. I start walking in Alex's direction, but just then an old man stops me. "I've never seen you around here before."

"Oh, I'm not from this city." I smile at the man, but I would like to get to Alex.

"Well, come on then, tell me your name! And what brings you here?" The old man begins talking my ear off. Going to see Alex seems impossible now. After my conversation with the old person, I decide to continue mingling around with people at the party.

'It's probably for the best that I don't talk to any of them right now. I'm still confused and hurt because of whatever happened.'

I head towards the lovely string quartet to watch them play. 'I wish music like this still was popular back in my land.' Listening to them, I feel as if I never wants to hear the music I am used to listening to back home. I continue to enjoy my evening.

'This is exactly how I pictured a ball being!'

Even though I haven't talked to Alex or Jack yet, I am still having a good time tonight. I turn around to find more people to talk to. There is a gorgeous woman vampire and she seems to be looking right at me.

'Is she coming over here?' The vampire starts heading towards me. I am intimidated by her gaze! Not sure about what she wants. 'I've to be more careful after what happened with Dawn, before she can reach me, I turn and walk to other direction. It doesn't take long for me to lose her. I eventually talk to all the humans and creatures the entire evening, the conversations are very distinct and interesting.

After a while I finally seem to have a moment to myself. That's when I spot Alex approaching me, but I'm not sure if I'm ready to talk to him yet. I turn and run away from Alex.

I see some doors leading out to the back, so I head through them and find myself in the garden. I duck behind some bushes. 'I don't think he'll be able to find me here.'

While hiding, I see a group of three women talking to each other animatedly. "I know, nearly fell off of my broomstick!"

"I could imagine! Those new designer cauldrons do not come cheap."

I overhear their conversations and realize they are witches. That's when I see them step closer together, their conversation seems to become more private.

'I wonder what they could be whispering about.' I stick my ear out to hear them better. The witches are talking in low, excited voices.

"Of course it is true! Can you believe it?"

"How can it be? Why now?"

"After all this time?"

"There are many questions to be answered still, but those don't matter now. All that matters is that it happened."

'What are they referring to?'

"My goodness.... The los princess."

"I can't believe she's finally here."

"When did you say she arrived?"

The witches discuss the lost princess, I almost remember reading some information about her in the Lord Eden family book. That's when one of the witches tells them about the day the lost princess apparently come to Night city.

'Oh my god!' I feel my heartbeat rise as I realize the day the lost princess arrived in the night city is the same day I was transported here too.

All the things start making sense now, but at the same time confusion takes over me. 'Does that mean... That I am the lost princess?'

Chapter 11

'Why am I so confused?' So far I've managed to find bits and pieces of different information, but it's difficult to put them all together. Night city is just as mysterious as Magical.

I slowly approach the three witches, they instantly turn their heads to me with a surprised look on their face.

"Why, hello there."

"I couldn't stop myself, I accidentally overheard your conversation—"I'm about to ask them who the lost princess is, but then Alex appears beside me. "Alex!"

"I've been looking for you, Claire!" Alex politely greets the witches and turns to me, his eyes filled with admiration. "You look beautiful tonight."

"Thank you." Alex gulps and holds his arm out for me. I exactly know what he's hinting at. "Shall we dance? I haven't forgotten the promise I made. To catch you before you fall!"

"I'd love to dance with you Alex"

***

I take his arm and go to the dance floor full of twirling couples. "Are you nervous?" Alex waits for my answer but instead, I bite my bottom lip and nod at him. He takes a deep breath, clearing his throat while staring at me. "Maybe a little."

Alex reaches out for my hands and places them in his big strong hands. He gently pulls me closer. I rest one of my hands on his shoulder and holds his other hand in mine. Alex begins leading me around the dance floor. He makes it incredibly easy and I feel just as talented as the other dancers on the floor.

"You're a natural!"

"I couldn't do it without you." The tension in the room is too much to take in. His hand rests on my shoulder and I look deep into his eyes as they stare back at me with a look full of burning desire. His eyes never leave me. Alex continues twirling me. The air is different and I can't stop smiling.

"While I have you here, I've been meaning to talk to you about something."

"Is everything okay?" Alex slightly chuckles. 'Wait...Is Alex ... Nervous about something?'

"Everything is wonderful. Having you here has been... incredible."

"Alex... I've loved every minute spent we've spent together."

"I feel the exact same way Claire. I can't deny that truth any longer." Alex gulps and intensively looks into my eyes. He cups my face with his hands taking a deep breath. "I'm falling for you, Claire." I stop dancing as Alex completes his sentence.

Emotion takes over me and I feel as if everyone else in the room has vanished, leaving just the two of us. I stare into each other's eyes, my heart beating faster than it ever has. Alex's hand trails down to my neck, he then leans in for a kiss. His lips look so inviting and delicious it's hard to resist, I want to kiss him too.

I clasp Alex's neck in my hands and lean in. Alex presses his lips to my. The feeling of my lips clashing onto each other is full of ecstasy. There's passion and lust in the air and neither of we moves to break away. 'I wonder what this could've led to if it weren't for these people around us.'

"You have no idea what I would do if we weren't in a room full of people." Alex said while breaking the kiss.

"Are you sure you can't read minds?" Alex kisses me again, his tender touch makes my knees grow weak. I wrap my arms around his neck, pulling him into a deeper kiss, my enthusiasm surprises him. Alex instantly kisses me back with the same hunger.

Jack walks straight at me, he doesn't seem to acknowledge Alex standing next to me. His eyes are fixated on me, his gaze is fiery. "Jack?"

"Mind if I cut in?" Jack steps closer to me abruptly taking my hand and pulling me away from Alex before we two could process it. He flips me over, making me face him as he asks to dance with me. 'Oh my god.' I gasp as I feel tingles when Jack's hands are on my body.

"I look absolutely stunning." I nervously chuckle at Jack's compliment, swooning in his arms. "I couldn't find you this morning."

"I didn't know you planning on leaving so soon." I take a deep breath, feeling a little dizzy and hot from all the dancing. As if he could read my thoughts, Jack stops and holds out his hand for me. "Come. Let's get some fresh air out in the terrace."

"That sounds perfect."

***

We two take a seat on a stone bench in front of a beautiful fountain. Jack looks into my eyes. His face darkens as he yearns for me. I nervously bite my lip unable to not stare at his perfect lips. "Jack, I…" He cups my cheek with his hands. "I don't like seeing you with Alex, Claire. I have developed deep feelings for you, no matter how hard I tried not to."

My heart leaps at his words. "I know you feel something for me, too. We wouldn't be sitting here like this if you don't."

"Jack, I—"

"I want to protect you from Alex. I need you to trust me when I say he's dangerous."

"Jack I am aware of the way I feel about Alex but I think I need to decide if I want to trust him."

"If you must. I only want to help you. I promise."

"I believe you." Part of me wonders if the only reason I found myself in the arms of Jack in the first place is because Alex somehow pushed me to him. 'Alex wasn't the one to save me from Dawn. And he didn't even seem worried when I made it back to his castle.' "I'm glad you're here with me, Jack."

"Me too." I gently smile at Jack yearning for his lips to meet mine.

Just when my lips are about to touch, I put my hand on his chest stopping him. "I'm sorry Jack." I stand up, feeling incredibly overwhelmed. "Where are you going?"

"I should go." Before I can do anything else, I see Alex storming out into the terrace, his eyes full of hatred as he approaches me and Jack.

"Alex!"

"Get inside Claire! Now."

"Alex! No." Alex turns to look me in the eyes. His gaze is full of anger but plead too...

"I'll explain everything to you shortly. Just please wait for me inside."

I watch the vampire brothers have their face off, I feel hopeless not knowing how to stop this from happening. 'I can't believe it! Before the ball, I thought I was invisible to both of them! And now they're standing here ready to fight each other over me?'

I step between the brothers and put one hand on each of their chests, hoping to separate them. "Jack! Alex! Please don't do this."

"Please. Claire. You don't want to see this."

"You're right, I don't!"

"There's a lot you still don't know." Without another word I leave the two of them alone. Afraid of what Alex and Jack are going to do to each other, I race back into the ballroom.

'Can someone here help me to get away?' I walk through the crowd of people, I hear a group of people discussing where Alex and Jack are. It makes my heart sink. I mask my feelings and plaster a fake smile on my face. "Tessa..." I spot Tessa sitting on one of the corner tables, the instantly looks back at me and gives me a warm smile.

"Hi again! I was wondering where you disappeared to." Her genuine concern lifts up my mood for a split second. I take a deep breath and ask her for the favor. "Do you think we could go somewhere? I just really need to get out of here."

"Of course. We can go to my house."

I and Tessa walks to her house. "I can't wait to get out of this dress, anyway."

"Yeah, same."

"Do you want to talk about what happened?"

'I'd love to have a friend to talk to about all of this, but I'm not sure I can trust her yet.' "Nothing really, I was feeling stuffy there with ball and everything."

"It's definitely a lot to get used to." I smile at Tessa and continue walking to her house, talking and learning more about her.

I arrive at Tessa's modernly designed house. Tessa takes me to her closet and tells me to pick out some clothes. "Are you feeling any better yet?"

I have so many thoughts and questions still racing through my mind.

"Maybe you should rest?"

"I have this one particular question burning a hole in my brain."

"Maybe I can answer it?"

"Well, it's about the lost princess. Do you happen to know anything about that?" I tell Tessa all the things I heard about the lost princess. "Is it just a coincidence that we arrived on the same day?"

"I wish I could tell you, but I'm sorry. Come with me. I might not know a whole lot about the lost princess, but maybe we can find you something to drink?"

We two head over to a café in the human part of the city, I nervously sip on my cup of tea. "You need to eat something."

"I guess, I'll try."

"What's up with you? You seem even jittery here than you were back at my place."

'It's so nice to have a friend. Tessa seems like she genuinely wants to make me feel better.'

"I'm just… feeling on edge, I guess." Tessa rolls her eyes, giving me a look of disbelief. Food arrives at our table shortly after, "Alright, Tessa. You've officially earned my full trust."

"Ah that sounds great! What do I win?" I'm amazed at how much better I'm feeling after I've had a couple of bites. "How much time do you have?"

"All night."

I tell Tessa everything that has happened between me, Alex and Jack since I arrived here in Night City. I even fill her in on my boyfriend, James, Back home. To my amazement, Tessa remains completely nonjudgmental of my choices.

"It looks like you really care for both of them. I know you are a little mad right now, but before you make any big decisions, you really need to think through my feelings. Everyone has flaws. Even vampires."

"You're right Tessa!" 'I am so glad I found her.'

"I think I am ready to turn in for the night."

"Me too." I and Tessa stand and walk outside. "So where am I walking you, now that you've had some time to calm down and think?"

"I'm not ready to see either of them. Would it be okay for me to stay with you tonight?"

"Yes! Of course Claire."

I and Tessa head back to her house. She has a spare room already set up for me. When I crawl under the covers, I'm amazed at how comfortable Tessa's mattress is. I'm ready to wind down, and after a few moments of twisting and turning, I finally drift off to sleep.

***

I'm hanging out in the café Tessa showed me yesterday, having some coffee and reading a book I snuck out of Alex's library. 'I still have to figure a way out of here all on my own.' The doorbell to the café chimes, Alex walks inside, looking dashing and making my stomach flip. I bury my nose in my book, a shadow appears over my head.

"Is this seat taken?" I giggle as he slides into the booth across from me. "I'm glad I found you, Claire."

I know Alex won't mind that I'm here alone because it's daytime and there are plenty of people around me. "What brings you to this part of the city?"

"Well, I guess you could say I'm here for business."

"What kind of business?"

"To get you home. But it would involve doing something I never wanted to do."

"Based on how uncomfortable you seem about it! I am going to tell you no." Alex chuckles and fidgets with his silver ring. "It's just that... I really think it could work."

"Alex, what is the idea? Can you at least tell me?"

"Okay, it's going to sound crazy, but it might be our only option."
" Go on!"

"I didn't want it to come to this, Claire, but I think we might not have another choice."

"What is it Alex?"

"I will need to feed on you."

My Ears can't seem to believe what they just heard. 'Alex wants to feed on me? Of course, I know that feeding on humans is how he survives, but I just wasn't expecting it... '"Wow."

"I know it may sound crazy, but at this point, I am starting to run out of other ideas."

"'Crazy' is a good word to describe that idea. But so is 'Intriguing'."

"You think so?"

"I've always thought so!" Alex adjusts himself in his chair, ready to get serious about the conversation. "I've been doing a lot of research."

"Is that so?"

"Yes. From what I have read, if I feed on you, I might become stronger, and be able to do things I couldn't otherwise." I don't say anything because I have too many thoughts running through my mind. "I know I said that I would never do this to you."

I recall the incident of Alex feeding on that women and the promise he made to me on that day. "I just want to be able to help you get back home, Claire. This is the only way that is safest to do it."

"Safest? Are you sure?"

"Yes. So what do you think? Will you try it?"

"I honestly think this could work, Alex. We should do it." Alex looks shocked. "Really?"

"Yeah. I mean, I've been trying to know what it feel like, you told me it feels like the best sex you've ever had. So, I'm a bit curious."

"This is great news, Claire! I am so glad you're on board." I feel a little bit nervous, but are excited about the feeling nonetheless. "I have one condition, Alex."

"You name it."

"You can't drink enough from me to bind us together." 'If I am going to feel forever drawn to Alex, I want it to be because of my own decision.'

"Of course. I wouldn't want that."

"When do we start?" Alex stands from the table and holds his hand out to me. "How about now?" I smile and take his hand, and the two of us rush back to Alex's castle.

Instead of lingering at all inside the halls of the castle, Alex immediately takes me up to his bedroom. 'Alex seem eager. Should I be more concerned?'

"Lie down here on my bed." I find my heart racing against my will, but I try to relax myself knowing that Alex will never hurt. "How are you feeling?"

"I am scared. I don't want it to hurt badly."

"Do you really think I would ever do that to you?"

"I don't know... Alex. I 've never done it before."

"I've been a vampire for a very long time. I promise I can control myself." Alex leans in very closer to me and whisper in my ear. It tickles my skin and sends Goosebumps across my body. "Just close your eyes and relax." I do as Alex says.

First, Alex's lips press against the crook of my neck. He is sweet and gentle and instantly makes my insides flood with desire for him. "Mnnmmm." Then suddenly, I feel a sharp pinch, but before my brain can even process the pain of it. My entire body is convulsing with pleasure. 'Oh my god! This does feel as good as amazing sex!'

I moan loudly and wiggle on the bed as Alex drinks from me. I couldn't be any quieter if I tried. "Alex!" He sinks his teeth further into me, sucking my blood, noises of pleasure sounding in the back of his throat.

'I feel like I'm floating! I feel like I am about to have the best orgasm of my life! Alex's fangs could rip me right open and I would still feel incomplete ecstasy.' Moans keep escaping my mouth, as pleasure floods over me. 'I don't know what Alex's thinking, but I do know that I am going to want so much more of him after this.'

When Alex finally forces himself to pull away, I feel myself getting closer to the climax. I desperately went Alex all over my body. "Are you okay? I open my eyes and look at Alex, my blood all over his mouth.

I nod, as Alex notices my healing scar. "It heals instantly. Let's clean you up." I grasp his biceps firmly. "No! Alex." I pull Alex back down to me. 'I don't want this incredible feeling to fade.'

"Are you sure?" I nod my head at him, pressing my lips against his. I find myself drowning in this ecstasy, making out with Alex was even better right now. "Oh my god, Claire."

He instantly leads his hand to my neck slowly choking me. I moan in pleasure. "Alex, I want more..." I feel different, demanding things from Alex, but knowing he was powerless when it comes to my blood, instilled a new dominating feeling inside of me.

Alex rips my shirt open easily tearing off the sexy black corset I am wearing underneath. Then he pulls back for a second admiring my naked body, I launch myself at him, kissing him again. "Alex!" Alex pushes me back down on the bed stripping my skirt and panties off of me. Then undressing and revealing his glorious naked body.

One of his hands finds its way to fondling my sensitive breast with his thumb and pointer finger. His other hand goes right to my throbbing, soaking core, "Alex! Fuck that feels so good!"

Alex kisses me on the lips, his tongue asking for access. "You taste so good, Claire!"

"Yeah?" I sit up and force him away from me, with a teasing look in my eyes. "Well I want to know how you taste." I push him back on the bed and gaze at his massive erection.

Eagerly, I take as much of him as I possibly can into my craving mouth. Alex gasps as his tip hits the back of my throat, making me gag slightly. He groans tugging on my hair tightly. It's as If the slight pain of Alex's fangs biting into me has made me suddenly obsessed with feeling pain and pleasure at the same time.

'What is the matter with me?' Alex takes me by the throat, only applying light pressure. "I can't hold back Claire."

"Then don't!" I moan in excitement and biting my bottom lip. Alex stares at me hungrily, growling and bending me over the arm of his chair. "Take me, Alex." Alex's hand swiftly smacks my waiting behind. The sting feels so good to me. "Alex, don't stop!" Alex makes my sex quiver with need.

"You're perfect Claire." Alex grabs hold of my hips and spread my legs apart, then he uses his hand and guides his manhood deep into my waiting void. We both moan at the same time as Alex thrusts deep inside of me.

"Claire what do you do to me!"

"You're amazing!" 'I can't get enough, is this what ecstasy feels like?'

"Will you come for me, Claire?" I nod my head and reach behind me to take his hand guiding it to my wanting core. He rubs in small, gentle quick circles continuing to thrust in me. The climax builds up until suddenly, I erupt, screaming out and clawing at the fabric of the armchair with an intense amount of strength it only takes seconds longer for Alex's body to do the exact same.

A little after Alex fed on me, we two fully dressed up fully clothe and the blood is cleaned up, Alex seems incredibly energetic. "I don't know how to describe it, Claire! It's as if my entire body is humming with electricity!"

"So it worked? Do you feel more powerful than before?"

"Yes, most definitely." I smile at him devilishly "Why don't you show me, then?"

"Do you mean I should test out my abilities?" I nod my head excitedly. Alex grins, he suddenly races around his bedroom, moving so quickly that I can barely see him. Objects of his go flying about, and so do chunks of wood from his furniture and maybe even some concrete particles from his bedroom walls.

"This is amazing!" I giggle, happy to see him letting loose and having so much fun. As I sit there and watch Alex soak in the glory and invincibility of his new powers, I am so caught up in him that I don't even notice it at first.

There's a tingling sensation flooding through my veins. I finally notice it and stop looking at Alex, I nervously look down at my own body, instead. 'Whoa, what is happening to me? It feels almost as if I can sense how much stronger my blood is making Alex. This doesn't make any sense!'

"Are you okay?" I look back at Alex and smile.

I'm not sure if this new feeling is something that is supposed to happen, or if I am having some sort of reaction to Alex feeding from me. 'I don't know if I should tell him, in case it worries him.' Instead of saying anything, I just quietly stare at myself in wonder.

For some reason, I start feeling more connected to being here than the world I came from. 'What if I don't want to come back?' "Alex, I'm just going to go into my room for a moment, I'll be right back." Alex flashes me a genuine smile as I walk up to the door leading to my room.

'I just need to figure out this feeling! Could I really be somehow gaining powers from Alex's bite? This is crazy. There's no way I have powers.'

I walk over to my small, but heavy nightstand made of solid wood. I push the edge of the nightstand easily sliding it across the wooden floor as if it weighed nothing. "OH MY GOD!"

Alex hears me cry out from the other room and calls out to me. "Claire, is everything okay?"

"Everything is great!"

I tell Alex that I want to head back into town. He doesn't seem pleased to see me leave, but he kisses my cheek goodbye anyway. I changed my clothes and walked out of the castle.

When I knock on Tessa's door, she lets me inside excitedly. "I am so glad you came back!"

"Of course I was going to!"

"That's great then! What would you like to do?" I and Tessa sit at her dining table. "There's actually one more reason I decided to come see you."

"Oh, what is it?"

"So, I know this sounds crazy, but Alex fed from me today and now for some reason I feel stronger than I ever was."

"What? That's not possible!"

"I know! And yet, it happened!" I pick up Tessa's dining table with ease showcasing my new powers. "Oh my god, Claire!"

"I might need to talk to the witches I overheard at the ball. I want to get to the bottom of this."

"I am not sure how I can help you figure all of this out!"

"I know you can help, Tessa. You know this city much better than I do."

"So what do you say I do?"

"I need you to give me direction to where the witches live."

"What!"

"You don't have to come with me! I just have no idea where to find them."

"That's too dangerous, Claire! Witches aren't very pleasant beings."

"I am willing to do whatever it takes to figure out what's going on. Please tell me where I can find them." Tessa sighs heavily. "Yes, I know where. But I can't let you go alone."

"So you'll come with me?"

"I guess so."

***

Tessa leads me to a small cottage in the middle of the forest as the sun sets around me. "This is it." I am suddenly reminded of the cottage dawn held me, hostage, in. It makes me shudder in fear. 'I can't let my fear interfere, I need to be brave.'

"Are you ready?" I nod my head taking a few steps forward. 'Why do I feel as if someone is staring at me through the trees?' I step towards the old wooden door and knock on it.

All the witches answers together. "Tessa! What a pleasant surprise!" "What is she doing with you?" "I recognize her from the ball!" I behave just the right way to get these witches to tell me what I've been dying to know.

"I am really sorry to disturb you, ladies, this evening…"

"What kind of questions?"

"Um… questions about the lost Princess?"

"How do you know about her?"

"Please, let us inside, and I'll explain everything." The witches all look at each other shooting looks. The main witch nods her head, and they all step aside letting me and Tessa inside.

I, Tessa, and the witches gather around a large wooden table. "How can we know if we should trust you?"

"I promise, I mean no harm."

"I say we read her palm! That'll tell us." Tessa looks extremely uncomfortable.

The witches have I sit in a chair as they bustle around the room and prepare themselves for my palm reading. Tessa lingers nervously in the corner. "Are you ready to have your future revealed?"

"Yes." The witches gather around me, the main one holding my hand open in hers. They all chant in Latin, then one of them speaks what they see. "You will achieve your greatest desire. You were born to be successful and strong. You will shortly fall in love with someone… it's going to be full of passion." Everything the Witches tell me about my future fills me with confidence. Afterwards, the witches look a little happier. "She is no danger to us. I suppose we can give her some information."

"Thank you so much!"

The witches launch into their explanation about the Lost Princess. "The missing vampire princess was from the strongest vampire family, the Eleazar's, she went missing years ago"

"How many years." Second witch rattles off a more specific time frame. 'Wait… that's exactly the time I was dropped off at the orphanage with absolutely no memory of my biological parents! Oh my gosh… this is happening…' "I think… I am the lost princess!" The witches laugh hysterically

"Yeah right! You have to be a vampire with incredible powers, my dear."

"I don't know how to explain it, but I think I do have those powers."

"Your powers wouldn't be activated until you've been bitten by a vampire for the first time."

"I was. Today! Alex fed on me, and now I have super-strength!" The witches and Tessa all gasp together, staring at me in amazement. 'I'm really the Lost Princess?'

Chapter 12

I feel surprised by learning truth. It sounds unbelievable to everyone but I'm The Lost Princess. 'At the same time, I don't feel that surprised at all. It makes so much sense. That's why I feel so strong now! And also the reason I felt so connected o Night City!'

I calmly stand up from my seat and take in a deep breath. "This is an interesting turn of events." 'No wonder I don't have any memories of my parents! My memory was erased when I was sent to the other land!'

"Oh my gosh, Claire. I can't believe this." I try my best to maintain my composure to prevent myself from freaking out. "Everything makes more sense now."

"How so?"

"Ever since I got here, I have felt…connected to Night City. And everyone in town seemed to connect with me too. I felt like I belonged here."

"It's so hard to believe that the lost princess is finally here, standing right in front of us." Tessa quickly approaches me and takes my hand. "Okay, Claire. I think it is time for us to leave."

"You don't have to go anywhere. We have so many questions we would like to ask you! Stay for tea!" "Won't you?" Tessa smiles nervously at the witches.

"I'm sorry, but we really must get going." Before I can ask the witches anything else, Tessa drags me out of their cottage and into the dark forest.

"Tessa, why does it seem like something is bothering you?"

"This is dangerous situation you have put yourself in. I don't think you seem to realize."

"What do you mean? How is it dangerous?"

"No one else can know about this, okay? It is already bad enough that those three witches know. I have to keep this a secret." Tessa looks so serious and worried that an uneasiness settles over me.

"Tessa, I don't think I have anything to worry about. This is good news, isn't it?"

"I don't think it is, Claire."

"But I have powers now and I am strong enough to protect myself."

"Maybe. But we don't know that for sure. You need to look out for yourself. This news is huge and could be potentially devastating, no matter how happy you feel about it right now." I sigh and slowly nod my head at her.

'I know Tessa is worried, but I can take care of myself now.' Tessa begins walking, but then she abruptly stops turning back to me. "Listen to me Claire. It's very important that you go back to Alex's castle and stay there. At least until we have everything figured out. Okay?"

"Won't you come with me?"

"There is something I have to do." I tilt my head at Tessa, not liking the idea of her being alone in these woods. Tessa seems to notice my concern. "You don't have to worry about me. I'm not the one that is in potential danger at the moment. See you, Claire." Tessa quickly hurries away, leaving me alone in the woods.

'I wonder what dangerous things Tessa thing could happen. I hope I get to Alex's quickly so that I can ask him.' I continue walking. Suddenly someone attacks me from behind. I'm shown to ground without any warning, screaming as I fall. When I turn back around, I see Dawn. She looks wild and angry and ready to take me down.

"Dawn!" I stay on the ground where Dawn shoved me. 'Maybe if I don't attempt to fight her, she will leave me alone. A magical light shoots out of her fingertips and hits me in the stomach, I slide across the forest floor with great force until I slam into the base of a tall tree.

'This hurts…' "What do you want from me, Dawn?!" Dawn walks in my direction hovering above my crumpled body on the ground. "I followed you to those witches' cottage. I heard everything you said to them."

I feel my heart pounding and my breaths becoming shorter. "I don't see why it concerns you!"

"You are the lost princess, it has to concern me! I want you out of Night city, Claire! You have two days."

I laugh at Dawn to show her that she doesn't scare me. "I think you keep forgetting something, Dawn. I have Alex to protect me. When I am with him, you can't touch me."

"I'd be worried for you!"

"What are you talking about?"

"Did you not listen to my little friend back there? You being the Lost Princess puts you in grave danger. If you don't leave Night city before the two days are up, I will tell the master who you are, and trust me, that is the last thing you want to happen."

I feel more nervous than I was when Tessa had warned me of the danger I was in. 'I didn't realize the vampire master- whoever that is- would see me as a threat!' "I don't believe a word of what you're saying to me."

I know deep down I'm lying to Dawn and myself. I would rather not find out what is going to happen if I don't leave in the next two days. "Just wait and see. Go back to your little castle with your little precious little Alex."

I turn and start to walk away from Dawn, but her next word make me freeze and turn back to her. "Who doesn't even love you, by the way?"

"What did you just say to me?"

"It's true. He knows who you are, he's just using you. With the Lost Princess by his side, he knows the power he has. He is aware you will get him high status he needs once the word gets out. He doesn't actually care about you." I ball my fists at Dawn, feeling my blood curl up. But instead of trying to fight Dawn or continue arguing with her, I turn and keep walking. I know Tessa told me to go back to Alex but my run-in with Dawn and the things she told me about Alex makes me want to think things over.

I go to look back at Dawn, but she suddenly is nowhere to be found. I am alone in the woods again.

I decide to keep walking, but I aren't sure where I should really go. 'If Tessa trust Alex, maybe I should too. But I just can't help the way I feel. Did Alex lie to me about everything? If I just keep walking, maybe my heart will lead me to the right place.'

It's getting later in the evening as I walk through the forest. "What am I going to do? Where am I going to end up?" 'There is one person I have in my mind.' "Jack!"

Suddenly, I know exactly where I'm headed. 'This might be the right choice after all! I just want to speak to Jack. Maybe he will know the truth about Alex and everything happening to me.'

My new abilities seem to include speediness as well as strength, I quickly find myself at the gates of Jack's dark castle.

I enter the castle but he's nowhere in sight. I walk further into the castle and eventually find him in his study poring over copious amounts of books. "Jack?" jack turns to me with a start. He hadn't even heard me come in.

"Claire! It's so good to see you. Wait a minute. What happened?"

'He might've been able to tell I'm upset somehow!' I step further into the study. "I had another run-in with Dawn." Jack looks deeply upset by this news. "How did this even happen? Were you in the forest alone again?"

"Not all night. Some of it, yes." I tell Jack everything Dawn said to me, except the part about me being the Lost Princess.

"I don't understand. Why would dawn want you to leave so badly? Why does she seem to think Alex will gain power and status by having you around?" I bite my bottom lip, nervous that Jack might figure out the answer. Jack's eyes widen with the realization of who I really am.

"Claire, you're the Lost Princess, aren't you?"

"Does that change how you feel about me?"

"This is quite the big news, but no, of course not. I am just trying to understand the connection between everyone. The witches, Dawn, Alex. It's a lot to process." I nod my head and sit in a chair. I am still feeling sad and overwhelmed. Jack gets up from his deck and sits in the chair next to mine. "Are you alright?"

'No I'm not! Everything is falling apart! As much as I would like to break down right now, I have to stay strong.' "Yes, of course. Don't worry about me. I'm fine."

"I don't believe that. You don't have to hide from me Claire." Jack instantly starts rubbing my back in a comforting manner. "We're going to figure all of this out, Claire." I nod my head, but at Jack's electrifying touch, I find Goosebumps spreading across my body. His hands are making it a little bit easier to distract myself from what's happening.

I stand up from the chair even though Jack was still trying to rub my back. "I'm sorry jack. I'm really tired."

"I understand."

"I think I would just like to go to sleep if you don't mind me staying here tonight."

"I wouldn't want you going anywhere else." I say goodnight to Jack and walk up the stairs to my room for the night.

***

I wake up with a jolted start, confused at first as to where I am and what time it is. 'I'm still at Jack's! It's still dark out, must be the middle of the night.' I turn my head to my right and see that Jack is asleep in my bed next to me. 'When did he come up and lay next to me? I still haven't decided what I should do about Dawn and Alex!' I slowly move to get out of the bed.

I try to be as quiet as possible as I get out of my bed. I want to go sit somewhere where I can think about what my plan of action is going to be. 'Maybe I'll go to his study. It was nice and peaceful there.' I open the bedroom door, and it creaks loudly making Jack stir. "Where are you going?"

"I am sorry jack, I was trying not to wake you! I'm going to get some air." Jack yawns and sits up in my bed. Then he pats the seat next to him. "Anything I can help you with?"

"Maybe..." I explain everything to Jack. "I just don't know... maybe I should leave Night city as she wishes. I just don't know where I would go if Alex doesn't help get me back to my land..."

"Do you want to know what I think you should do?

"Yes, Jack! What do you think? Jack holds my hand. "You should stay here with me. If you stay here with me, you might as well help me win the election and not Alex." An uneasiness settles over me at Jack's words. "Are you really that concerned about the election right now?"

"Claire, it's important to me and my family! The results are going to be announced soon. We both know you're better off being on my side than Alex's. Who knows what my power hungry brother will do to Night City if he wins?!"

'I don't like of jumping back and forth between helping brothers. I don't think the townspeople would like it either. It's really weird that Jack is still obsessing about winning the election at a time like this. Doesn't he care more about the safety of the woman he loves? I need to find out why it's so important to him.'

"Jack?"

"Yes?"

"Do you want to know what I was thinking about last night in your study?"

"What was it?"

"I really wanted you to make love to me." Jack's eyes instantly grow hungry. He reaches over and begins stroking my bare thigh. "Is that so?"

"Mhmm. I can't stop thinking about it now as well..." I roll on top of Jack leaning in, centimeters away from kissing him, but then backing away quickly. "But you're too busy being concerned about the stupid election." Jack looks frustrated with the teasing I'm doing to him.

"You must know that I can't possibly be thinking about the election when you look like that and are riding on top of me."

Jack scoots closer and nibbles on my ear, desperate for me.

"Why do you care about it so much?" I turn my head and give him my most tender, loving, slow kiss. "I have to win. It's the most important thing to me. I must defeat my brother. It's all I care about." He dives in to kiss me again, but I push him off of me. "All you care about? What about me?" I get out of bed. "No! I didn't mean it like that. I'm sorry, Claire!"

"I should go."

"Fine. Go." I leave the bedroom and walk out of Jack's castle back into the dead of night.

***

I'm making my way through the forest as quickly as I can to get to Alex's castle. 'Maybe it's not Alex who I should be worried about. I don't think Jack has good intentions!' I feel stupid for thinking I could trust Jack. As I walk, I hear rustling in the trees in the distance followed by muffled voices.

I stop for a moment and see if I can make out what the voices are saying. 'I think I just need to move a little bit closer!' I take a step, but then I snap a twig under my foot, and the voices quickly stop. 'Oh no!' I duck behind a tree to avoid being seen by anyone, and after a long moment, the voices finally start back up again. I can hear what they are saying to each other.

"Besides, even if Alex does win, it won't matter."

"Why not?"

"I'll kill Alex so Jack gains the power anyway!"

'Oh my god! They're planning to kill Alex? Who are they?! I need to get to Alex!'

I rush inside Alex's castle trying to find him as quickly as I can. 'Where are you?' After a long while of pacing around looking for Alex, I surprisingly spot him in one of the dungeons. "Alex?" I see him kneeled down with his back turned to me, his eyes focused on something in front of him.

Alex's tall body frame makes it hard for me to see. 'What's that?' Alex snaps his head to me, startled he quickly wipes his eyes. 'Is Alex crying?' I step forward to ask him what's wrong, but that's when I catch a glimpse of the painting behind him.

"Um, Alex?" Alex sighs and turns away from the painting revealing it. A look of surprise washes over me as I finally take a look at the painting. The women in the portrait looks just like me, leaving me bewildered. 'I really want to know what all this is about. But I don't think I should question Alex right now.'

"How did you find me down here?"

"I needed to talk to you Alex." I take in a deep breath and turn myself into Alex's arms. "What is it Claire?"

"I am the Lost Princess Alex!" I nervously look at Alex, waiting for his next words but instead, he says nothing. "What happened?"

"You can't be the lost princess."

"But-"

"You're not!" Alex cuts me off in a demanding tone. His face is full of sadness and confusion. "How do you know?" Alex steps closer to me, still looking sad but no longer weeping. "Because of that women in the picture Claire. She was The Vampire Princess, She's not lost!"

"What do you mean?"

"She's dead. I held her in my arms the night it happened. She... you look so much like her. I find it hard to believe my own eyes sometimes." Alex's words leave me in utter confusion, I proceed to tell him all the information I've gotten so far and from the witches. "Alex, it was nothing but a lie! For you and everyone else to believe that the Vampire Princess died, they did that to protect her."

"You can't really think that, can you?"

"I'm almost certain of it, Alex! Because I'm the Lost Princess. I just know I am. It all adds up!" I race into his arms and gaze into his eyes, which are tearing up all over again. Finally, Alex's eyes fill with belief, his facial expressions relax as a tear rolls down his cheek.

"I'm here, Alex." Alex leans in and gives me a deep passionate, love- filled kiss. The kiss overwhelms me with sensation, making me grow weak in the knees, but Alex grips me tight and his skillful lips never leave mines. Suddenly, memories start flooding my brain.

'I don't believe it! I am remembering something. I used to lie here! This is my land. That painting is of me after all!' I break away from the kiss, not leaving Alex's embrace. "Wait, Alex!" Alex gently moves a small strand of hair away from me patiently waiting for me to say what's on my mind. "What is it Claire?"

"Did you... see those visions in your head too? The memories... of us?" Alex pulls me into a brief kiss again, grinning cheek to cheek.

"It really is you!"

"Someone sent me into a parallel world, and I couldn't remember any of this!"

"Do you remember everything?"

"A lot is still unclear, but it's starting to come back to me!"

"Claire you meant everything to me, I thought I lost you forever. And now you're back." Alex kisses me deeply, passionately, and even more intensely now than before. Instinctively, I claw at his back as his tongue asks for access. Alex groans and clings on to me more tightly. "Alex!"

"Let me stay close to you, I can't express how happy I am to have learned the truth." He leans in and kisses my neck, the sweet spot behind my ears, sending tingles all over my body.

"Can you take me back to your room, Alex?"

"Of course." Alex scoops me up in his arms lovingly, and carries me like a baby out of the dungeons. I find myself smiling as I hold myself close to him. 'I never want to be away from him, ever again.'

I wake up the next morning in bed with Alex's arms wrapped around me. He seems to be awake already, snuggling me. "Good morning." He smiles at me, his adoring expression makes my heart flutter. "Did you sleep well?" Alex holds his arm out. I scoot closer to him, laying my head on his bare chest. "Mostly yes. I just had one night mare…"

I proceed to tell Alex everything that Jack has been telling me lately, after I explain that my nightmare had been about him trying to hurt me. Alex seems deeply bothered and upset by his brother. I nervously sigh and wait for his response.

"I can't believe he is being like this. I don't know where we went so wrong…"

I snuggle Alex affectionately, reassuring him that everything will be okay. "I'm sure everything will work out for the best. You're better off without him Alex. He doesn't care about anything but himself and winning."

Alex gives me a reassuring squeeze on my arm and pulls me into his embrace. "You're right."

"You don't have to worry. You deserve to win the election. And I will be by your side… always." My words don't seem to affect Alex as his jaw tenses even more making him sound even more stressed. "Jack is going to be extremely wicked and dangerous if he doesn't win. It's hard to know what he will do."

'What is Alex getting at?' "Alex the people, they love YOU! Not him."

"I know, I'm just worried he might retaliate."

"Besides, we haven't talked much about me being the lost princess."

"What are you saying?" I give Alex a devilish smile and walk away from the bed. He looks confused but interest. "Let's just say that I am pretty sure I'll be able to tackle Jack." Alex kisses my cheek. "If you say so, beautiful." I swoon and look at Alex with love-filled eyes.

***

I make it down for breakfast, I can't help but notice Alex's worried expressions. "Do you have a big day today?"

"Yeah, I guess you could say that."

"I can tell you're worried, what's going on?"

"This campaigning is beginning to worry me, that's all."

"Alex, there's no way you're not going to win."

"Thank you, Claire! The final campaign rally is today. But I'm worried about you Claire. I cannot bear not having you in my sights. I'm not going to be able to concentrate properly without knowing you're safe."

'He worries so much about me...' "You don't have to worry so much! I'll come with you."

"I don't know. It might be safer for you here in the castle."

"It's better if I go with you. We will keep each other safe."

"You're right Claire. You should go get ready for the day."

I leave the dining room and enter my own bedroom. I open my wardrobe and try deciding on the best outfit for the day.

***

I and Alex arrive at the campaign rally. I can't help but look at all the people around. 'There are so many people here for Alex!' I give Alex's hand an exciting squeeze.

"Look at the love and support this city has to offer you."

"I can't believe it!"

'I am feeling more hopeful about this election than ever before.'

"I have to go talk to some people, but don't worry, you'll be safe." I turn around in hopes of finding a familiar face and I see the main person I want to speak to first is my dear friend Tessa. I spot her conversing with a different creature. "Tessa!" Tessa turns around as I call her out. She talks quietly so that no one will overhear. "Hello, my secret vampire friend."

"I've been practicing my powers!"

"I can't believe Alex drank your blood. Was it amazing?"

"What can I say? It was ecstatic." I and Tessa continue talking and catching up. I excuse myself to go check on Alex, but that's when I feel a hand grab me. I abruptly turn around to them.

"So what happened after I left you in the woods when we talked to those witches?"

"You scared me!" I fill Tessa in on my run-in with Dawn and the warning she gave me. Tessa's face looks alarmed. "What are you going to do now?"

"I told Alex I won't leave his side. I am sticking to my word."

"I knew you'd never pick the wrong side." Tessa gives me a friendly hug. "I am worried about you. I won't lie about it."

"Everything is going to be okay."

"If you believe, then so do I." I and Tessa talk and chat for a little while, then she slightly points me to a group of women I don't recognize. 'They look like normal humans.'

"See them?"

"Who are they?"

"They're the witches that support Alex! They will definitely answer your questions about the witch attack!"

"That's a great idea." I approach the group of kind-looking women. They turn around to greet me. "It's Claire! Hello!"

"We think Alex is wonderful!"

"And so are you!"

"You are so kind to say so. Thank you for coming. I actually had a question, if you don't mind?" I fill them in, while giving them as little detail as possible. "So how I might better protect myself?"

The witches start thinking deeply before one of them starts speaking. "Witches shoot spells out of their fingertips after thinking them strongly inside their heads."

"Your best bet is to confuse a witch, so they can't think about the spells clearly."

"Thanks to you all for your advice."

***

I and Alex head back to his castle after the rally, it was a tiring day and relaxing is all I can think of right now. Soon after the winner is also going to be revealed.

I take Alex's hands into mine, giving it a reassuring squeeze. "I'm so happy to have you here. I'm worried about the results."

"No matter what happens we are in this together Alex."

"I just want to make Night City a better place."

"I know you will get chance to."

When I and Alex returns to the town square later in the evening, it appears that all of the Night city is there to watch the results take place. "Alex this is so exciting!"

"Claire, will you come up on stage with me?"

"This is your time to shine, Alex. I'll be right here cheering you on." Alex grins at me, swiftly taking me in his arms. He gives me a deep and passionate kiss. 'Why is he so amazing?'

"I feel ready now." I giggle and watch Alex take his place on the stage next to Jack. The announcer walks up on the stage. "The votes have all been counted, and the results are in!" The crowd cheers, I feel myself becoming more and more nervous as the tension starts to build up. "Are you ready to hear who the winner is?"

Chapter 13

When I hear the news, I can barely believe my ears. Alex did it. He won! I clap my hands together loudly, cheering. People in the crowd begin to scream in joy as well. Poppers unleash confetti into the crowd as the cheers climb up and become louder. When I look at Alex, I feel myself Smile. "Alex, we did it! You won the election! I'm so proud of you!" He doesn't seem to hear me over the cries of joy from the crowd.

Alex spreads his arms out, and the audience continues to cheer for him. Suddenly, in the crowd I notice someone familiar. 'Is that Jack?' I narrow my eyes and look into the crowd, trying to figure out the shadow of the person.

I take in a deep breath and jus when I'm about to say something, Alex finally makes it to me. "There you are!" He picks me up quickly spinning me around, nearly squealing like a child himself.

When he finally lowers me, he plants several kisses on my forehead and cheeks. "This is not enough!" I trail my hands to Alex's shirt pulling him closer as I finally kiss him. "Better!"

"Aha! I love you Claire!" Alex kisses me again, it is full of passion and joy as his hands cradle my face. I feel the warmth of my body radiating near him, my heart pounding in my ears.

I remember the night he fed on me, and my entire body begins to tremble as I reminisce. I smile underneath the kiss as Alex finally pulls back, taking my hands in his. "We did it, Claire. I wouldn't be here without you. This is your victory as much as it is mine."

"Your win means the world to me Alex, I'm so happy for you." I wink at him, Alex licks his lips seductively just then the shadow from before appears at my side. Alex notices my frown and turns to see what is bothering me. 'Jack! I was right!'

"Can I talk to Claire? Alone?"

"Absolutely not! Stay away from her, Jack."

"Whatever it is, you can say it to the both of us."

"Claire please." Jack pleads with me, a tiny bit of guilt twinges inside me. I feel like I should hear him out.

"Don't force her to do something she doesn't want to do, Jack."

"I will talk to you alone if Alex can see me at all times. Is that fair?"

"Well...yes. Fine. I can afford to that!" Jack moves me to the side. Alex's eyes are fixated upon the two of us. I send a reassuring smile his way before turning to Jack. "Tell me what is it?" Suddenly, Jack's demeanor changes. His eyes are clouded with serious anger, and I take a few steps back. It doesn't scare me, but it definitely makes me uncomfortable.

I'm about to shout for Alex when Jack grabs my arm. "You may have won the election, but you won't last much longer. I will kill my brother in his sleep if I have to. This position is rightfully mine."

"You wouldn't hurt Alex."

"You don't know me Claire! I'll convince all of night city what an incompetent leader Alex is! That will embarrass our entire family line, and I will easily rise to power!"

"Jack, think of what you're doing. You're drawing a line in the sand here with family. Doesn't that mean anything to you?!" Jack laughs, letting go of my arm. "Oh Claire, I thought you knew my better than that. You can go back to the love of your love Claire."

I rush back to Alex as quickly as I can. I don't like the way Jack's gaze feels on me as I walk away from him. My wrist burns as I turn to Alex with pleading eyes. "Claire, did he hurt you?"

"I am glad we're done for the day, and it also ended with some great news." I plaster a fake smile on my face, to avoid Alex noticing my slightly bruised wrist.

"Claire, what did he say?" Alex's eyes instantly spot the small bruise on my wrist. His upper lip curls. "Did he do this? He has a death wish!"

"No! He didn't hurt me on purpose, Alex!" What happened back there?"

"He started saying scary things about hurting you, and grabbed my wrist. I'm sure he didn't mean anything to do it on purpose." Alex lets off a sigh. "Regardless, I don't want his hands on you. But I doubt I can really do much about it at this point. Where is he anyway?"

I follow Alex's gaze and he is absolutely correct. Jack is nowhere to be found. I don't know why this makes me so uneasy.

I feel myself being uneasy at all times, with that threat looming over my head. "Okay, why don't we celebrate this time together? I would hate for you to be worried all the time because of my brother."

"But Alex—"

"This is a celebration Claire, the victory is finally ours!"

"Are you sure you'll be alright?"

"Of course." Alex flashes me a reassuring smile, his warm behavior makes me feel at ease as well. "I'll be right back okay?" I smile back at him as he disappears into the crowd to shake some hands.

I turn and start walking into the crowd as well, trying to decide what to do. 'The only thing I want to do is feel Alex's body on mine.' I walk around for a while, shaking hands and dancing with a few of Alex's supporters. It wasn't hard for me to draw a crowd.

After what felt like hours, I search for Alex. The sun is beginning to set, and I still can't find him. "Alex! Where are you?!" There's no answer. I fret, worrying at my bottom lips as I wonder where he is. 'Did he already go home? Maybe he's waiting for me?'

I try convincing myself that everything is fine but the threats keep looming over my head, leaving me completely unsure about everything!

When I walk into the castle, I get a feeling that Alex has already been here. The servants stare at me with concerned eyes, as if they are hiding something. It makes me feel uneasy as I quickly rush to my room. 'Why do I feel like something is wrong?'

When I open my door, I find Alex lighting candles near the table, he's well dressed, looking his best! "Alex. How could you! I was so scared…" Alex stops and turns around, looking shocked. "My dear, I am sorry, but I couldn't find you either! I assumed you would come back home, so I wanted to give you a surprise."

"I know, I'm sorry… I just …I'm just relieved that you're okay."

"Of course Claire, I am. Come here please, I can't hold anymore!" I chuckle and obey Alex, I run into his arms leaving no space in between the two of us. "I never want to be away from you, even for a second."

"You won't Claire, I promise!" Before I can say anything, Alex pulls me in for a tight, passionate kiss. It is full of pure lust and love. His bare chest presses against my shirt as his lips part, teasing me with his tongue.

When he pulls away, I find myself breathless. "Claire I am truly flattered that you stayed by my side. I couldn't be more grateful to have you with me." I sit by him at the fire, as the two of us enjoy each other's company. "This is nice and warm, Alex. I appreciate it."

"Well, I didn't make this nice fire and candlelight area just for fun. I do have one particular goal in mind."

"Oh yeah? And what's that?" Alex takes in a deep breath, his hands cupping mine. His eyes look serious with a little hint of mystery, it draws me in even more. "Claire, you have no idea how long I've waited for you. I missed you so much!" he runs his fingers through my hair. "Having you back is like finding myself again. I can't... and I won't... lose you again."

"You won't Alex, I promise!"

"Please don't leave my side." Emotions overtake me. Alex never talked to me like this. I have no idea what I did to get this lucky... I pull Alex in for a kiss, and he instantly kisses me back. "I love you, Alex!"

"I love you too, Claire!"

It seems Alex has better plans. He gently lays me down, kissing my neck, lifting my shirt over my head and kissing my bare breasts, causing my breath to hitch. Little moans escape my lips. "Ah! Alex!" Before I know what's happening, Alex props me on the bed, leaning between my legs. His tongue traces my entrance, and I cry out in anticipation.

He wastes no time, going down on me with enough ferocity to cause any women to come within seconds.

I scream with pleasure as his tongue flicks over my entrance to my clit, going back and forth and back and forth... I come so hard, I see spots in my vision. My entire body trembles as I scream loud enough for the whole castle to hear.

I don't stop convulsing for a long time, Alex's hands on my thighs as my heart beat jumps into the air. "Oh Claire, you look so beautiful when you come." His filthy compliments make me blush hard.

"Alex! It would be better if we stop."

"Sure Claire, whatever you say…" Alex kisses my forehead and wraps his arm around me.

As the sun goes down, I lie in Alex's arms. I feel myself about to fall asleep, listening to the sounds of his breathing in my ear.

Suddenly, as I'm about to slip into unconsciousness, I hear shouting from outside. "Do you hear that?"

"What's wrong, Claire?" I bolt up, Alex is already on his feet, scrambling to get dressed. To my horror, I hear someone scream down the hall.

"THE CASTLE IS UNDER ATTACK!"

Chapter 14

Walking into the room, I see many suits of armor waiting to be worn. They range from very basic all the way to containing magic.

Alex comes in while I debate on which one to choose. "Claire, I wanted to talk to you before we had to do this."

"What is it?" I longingly wait for Alex's next words, his hesitant behavior worries me. "I love you."

"Alex…" Alex takes a deep breath. Taking my hand in his, his eyes are full of genuine compassion. "Claire… There is a chance we won't make it through this alive."

"No please." I run into Alex's embrace holding him tight. He wraps his arms around me as the two of us stand together in silence. "I believe in us Alex, I know we can do it."

"I only wanted to tell you that no matter what happens, if we don't make it through this alive, I love you." His words bring me to tears, but I try my best to hold them back. My heart doesn't agree with Alex, deep within I know saving this castle and this city from evil forces is my responsibility, I was born as vampire princess, I will never run away from what I was born into.

I look into Alex's eyes with admiration. He leans down and kisses my forehead. He steps away from me and takes leave. "I love you, Claire."

Using my power I track down Dawn's location, and I find out that she is the commander of the attack. If I kill her, it all ends.

I make my way towards her location and spot her hiding in the back, not wanting to get her hands dirty. "Why would you want others to risk their lives while you hide?"

"I'm only here for the grand finale baby. I don't have to worry myself with all this trivial fighting." I use her ego to distract her as I advance and get close enough to attack. "Dawn I know you don't want to admit you're scared."

"Ha! I took you down once, I won't hesitate to do it again." Dawn shoots me an evil glare, giving me enough time to make a move. I suddenly pounce on her, but her reflexes act fast and she runs away.

Dawn runs away as quickly as she could. As I run behind dawn, attempting to catch her I hear painful grunts coming from nearby.

A look of surprise washes over me as I recognize the two people in front of me. I see Alex and Jack aggressively fight each other.

I immediately run over them, to stop them. "Please Alex, don't lose hope." Alex regains his confidence and starts to fight for his life.

Jack's movements slow down and he starts bleeding from multiple wounds. Just as he is about to deal a deadly blow, Dawn shows up between them, clapping her hands together. A bright white light explodes from her palms and right into Alex.

When the light settles I am finally able to see, I instantly rub my eyes and spot Alex thrown at a great distance. "NO!" I run as fast as I can and hold Alex's head in my lap. "Alex, please open your eyes. Look at me" tears starts streaming down my cheeks.

I wait for Tessa to come help me. I gaze down at Dawn and Jack not knowing what they are going to try next.

"You are so pathetic. You really thought you could fight against super naturals and win?" Jack gives me a wicked smile, mocking my powers. "Even when I'm weak from fighting Alex, you couldn't kill me. He has taught you nothing the entire time you have been here."

"What did we ever do to you?" Jack laughs his evil laughter almost scaring me.

"I can still give you everything that he couldn't, Claire. Come with us to my castle and I will teach you how to truly be powerful."

"I will never join you, even if Alex was human, he is still better then you."

"If Alex ever wakes up that is, good luck with bringing him back to life. Dawn's joined forces with the most powerful witches."

"You don't have an honorable or noble bone in your body! When you knew you were going to lose, you cheated! No matter what happens, I will always love Alex. I will never be with you.

How can you even do this to your own brother?" Jack stares at me with a deathly glare.

"We will see. Don't come crawling to me when he fails you again." He laughs and walks away with Dawn following him.

I look down at Alex who does seem to be getting better. I manage to take him back to the castle

***

The cuts and bruises aren't nearly as bad as they once were, and Alex seems to be getting better, I get him into the bed. Prying open his mouth, I put my wrist against his fangs. "Drink so you can come back to me soon. I can't defeat both Jack and Dawn without you. We all need you Alex."

My blood heals Alex's wounds completely, although he hasn't woken up yet. Exhausted from the day, I take off my war outfit and lay down next to him. "I love you, Alex." Quickly, I drift off to sleep with my head resting on his shoulder.

A few hours later, I slowly wake up when there is shifting beside me. When I crack open my eyes, I find Alex awake. "You're up! Do you need anything, are you still in pain?"

"I am better now Claire, all the thanks to you. I don't know what I would do without you in my life."

"We're in this together Alex!"

"You care for me like no one else. I owe you a great debt that can never be repaid."

"All I care about is that you are alive." I lean over him to kiss his lips. His hands come up to rest on the back of my head, holding me close to him. His fingers intertwine in my hair, not leaving me for even a second. 'I almost lost him, I can't bear the thought of him being away for even a second now.'

Alex's hand roan down my body. His touch is light, he gently trails his hand to my hip, grabbing a hold of it tightly, and pulling me on top of him. I can't help but gasp at his gesture. "I don't want to hurt you." Alex flashes me a reassuring smile. "The only time I would be hurting me, is by leaving me alone right now."

I don't want to hurt him any more than he already is. As much as I want to keep going, I don't want to risk his health taking a bad turn. I give him one last peck on the lips and wrap my arms around him. "Do you need any more blood to help you heal?"

"You have given me more than enough for now. You need to get better as well. Let's call it a night and get some more sleep."

I wake up, feeling last night's defeat all over again, not sure if I'll get another chance to save the night city from the evil leader like jack and dawn, I'm deeply engrossed in thoughts just when I feel Alex come behind me. "We will win. Our people will be safe Claire, I don't want you worrying about anything now."

"You always understands me…"

"I want you by my side always."

"I'm so grateful to have you with me." Alex flips me over, making me face him. His hands cup my face, as he leans forward to place his lips on mine. 'I will never miss another moment to be with him again.' "I need to go see Tessa."

"I understand. Thank her for all the help she has provided."

"I will." I kiss him one last time before heading in to get ready.

***

"Come in! I am surprised to see you after last night." Tessa welcomes me in her house. "I couldn't wait to see you!" I follow her inside and sit on the couch in the front room.

Tessa brings me tea and I get ready to tell her everything. "How is Alex?"

"I'm just happy he's alive. I don't think he's fully healed yet. I am afraid Jack and Dawn will take advantage of us while Alex is in his weakened state. He said he wants me to join him, but even if Alex was gone, I would never choose to be with him." Tessa grows pale as she stares at me. "What is wrong?" I gulp down that sip of tea. It's hard to do with the lump in my throat. "This was isn't over yet!"

"Are you saying that...?" I stare at Tessa with a confused look on my face, unable to understand what Tessa's trying to get to. "What are you talking about?"

"Well look, think about Jack. Think about what you know about him. Consider this question: would he seriously let someone get in the way of him getting what he wants?"

"Have you seen this happen before?"

"Not with a women, no. he's never had anyone but Alex stand in his way. I'm just warning you based on what I know."

"Tessa, how did he turn so hateful towards his own brother?"

"It all began with the vampire princess, Jack felt played by her, well I mean by you."

"What?"

"I think both of them really loved her back then, and when she disappeared the bond between the brothers suffered greatly. Jack is only functioning on hate."

"I have to fight him back. It's only fair. This position belongs to Alex and me!"

"What's right and what's fair isn't always the same thing, you know."

"Just tell me how to beat him, Tess."

"Well... I can tell you the surefire way to kill a vampire has always been a stake to the heart. If you can get close enough to do that, that's one way to kill them."

"He'll never let me get that close to him. There has to be another way."

"Well... as the vampire queen, you could technically use your magic to kill him. You must harbor all your powers and take him down." I nod, thinking about all the possibilities to kill Jack. "How do I harbor all my powers?"

"When the witches sent you to the human world in disguise, they sealed your powers with true love, when you'll ignite the love within you'll be at your highest potential."

"So the key to unlocking my powers is in self-love?"

"That's right."

"Thanks again, Tessa! I should head back."

"See you soon! Stay safe. I hope I was of some help."

I head out of Tessa's front door, she waves at me bidding a goodbye. As I make my way down the path, I notice something moving in the forest. I look around myself, cautiously. I silently tip toe toward the person in the woods. The closer I get, the more certain I am that he is a human. The shadow looks like they're lost and looking around frantically. 'Who can that be?' I walk towards the shadow being completely aware that I might be putting myself in danger. "Oh my God! James?"

Chapter 15

"Claire?" I instantly run towards James, having a million questions running through my mind. "What the hell are you doing here, James!?"

"Oh, Claire! I missed you! I can't believe you're here!" James rushes to me and wraps his arms around me. Having his arms around I feel extremely foreign. I can't relate to the person I used to be with in the human world is now in this world. "James…"

"Oh my god, I missed you so much! I am so sorry for the way I've treated you in the past, really…. I can't wait to take you home."

"Home? Why would I want to go home with you, James?" James scoffs. "What are you talking about, Claire? Don't you want to come home? You were lost for months. I've been looking for you like a crazy person. Now that we've found each other don't you want to go home?"

"This is my home, now." James laughs. "There's no way that this place is your home. Your home is back with me, Claire. You know that."

"I know you heard me, James. You can't take me back home because I don't want to go back home."

"Why? What's so good about this place?" I don't answer it. 'How do I tell him I'm vampire princess, the human world was never my home. I always belonged here.' "It's better here than it was back home, James. This is where I belong. I hope you understand. And now you need to go back to where you came from. This place is not safe for you, James."

"No I don't! I was scared for you, Claire! I had no idea where you were or what happened to you-"

"The main question is, how did you even get here?"

"There was some wacky tunnel, I don't remember much."

"A wacky tunnel... you mean the portal?"

"Well, the point is I just fell in here."

The portal's reality shocks me, I can't believe it was always open. 'Did Alex lie to me about the portal?' "Listen babe, you know that we need to go home soon. This place seems dangerous, we don't belong here. Come back home with me, please. I promise I'll be better, I will."

"I'm not going anywhere until I talk to Alex. He has some questions to answer."

"Let me come with you! I don't want you getting hurt and nor do I want to be left alone here in the woods."

"You'll be fine. I have to see Alex, and you can't come with me. It's way too dangerous to take you with me."

"Claire, please! I have no idea what to do!" I pay him no attention as I make my way to Alex's castle.

I walk up to the castle silently, trying to think of what to say to Alex. I walk inside and spot Alex waiting for me, looking extremely worried. "Alex?" I call out to him, as he rushes to come see me. Alex wraps me in a tight hug, kissing my forehead. "Oh, Claire, where were you? Are you alright?"

"I just went to see Tessa, Alex I told you!"

"I know but I was worried, you were gone for too long. The danger isn't over yet, we lost a lot of our soldiers in the battle. We're still weak."

"I understand." I force a smile onto my face trying my best to keep Alex away from any suspicions. "Well, are you feeling better?"

"You looked worried Claire, are you sure you're feeling good?"

"Uh yes." 'Maybe I shouldn't have said anything after all... I can't accuse him after everything that he has done for me.' I decide that it isn't worth keeping to myself.

Taking matters in my own hands is necessary if I want to get some answers. 'If Alex kept the news about the portal from me, I need to be careful while getting the information from him.' I rush Alex suddenly, pulling him in for a surprise kiss. I can tell that it surprised him as he stumbles to catch me.

His mouth is soft as he kisses me back, kind and slow at first. I speed up the pace. I want him ravenous for me so I can get the answers I deserve. Alex moans, taking in this surprise kiss as he grips my waist. "Oh, Claire, did you miss me that much?" Panting, I pull back. "You know you've turned me insatiable."

"Oh, don't tempt me!" he begins making out with me with the same ferocity I started this make-out session with. My hands tangle in his hair as he slams me against the wall. My breath is knocked out of me, but I don't care. "Tell me what you want! I'll give it to you."

I whimper in Pleasure as Alex slides his tongue down the side of my neck. "Are you not able to form words to tell me how much you're enjoying yourself?" he hitches my legs up around his waist. I can feel his rock-hard abs and growing length against me. I whimper harder, spurring him on. He takes it in stride, continuing to make out with me. His hands are everywhere.

He's grabbing my thighs, my breasts, and my ass. I can't help but cry out in anticipation. 'I want him so bad, but I also need to get the answers from him.' "Alex, I need to ask you something." Alex stares at me, expectantly. "About the portal that brought me here."

Alex tenses. It's obvious that this isn't exactly something he wants to talk about, but I need to know. "How exactly did I get here?"

"Well, the portal let you in, as I told you before."

"Did the portal ever close?"

"Why do you ask that? Are you wanting to return home?"

"What? No, it's not that at all! It's just... well... Alex... someone from my old world showed up in the woods. It's so unexplainable considering the portal was closed." Alex frowns, he looks like he's thinking too deeply. "Well... truth be told, the portal is actually never open. It wasn't even a portal, to bring someone in the night city the witches perform a very big ritual when your time was to return here, the spell you read brought you here without anyone else's help." I don't hear the rest of Alex's rambling. Instead, I look straight ahead. 'If the portal was never open... then James is lying...' I go pale. 'Who bought James here?!'

"Claire, why are you suddenly talking about the portal? I can't lose you when I have just found you again."

'I have to do something, I can't let him know... I need to find why James is here without involving Alex.' "Well I just wanted to know!"

"Well if there is anything else, you know you can talk to me." That's the last thing I want. 'I hate lying to him, but I need to go check on James and make sure he is okay.'

"Alex I'd love to lay here with you all night but actually I do need to see Tessa about something I forgot."

"You just got back from seeing her. And you know it's not safe for you to be out there."

"I need to know something."

"What is so important that it can't wait till morning?"

"It's something about Tessa, I can't disclose it yet.

"Okay Claire, just be safe, okay?" He plants a kiss on my forehead in a tender way that makes me feel safe.

Alex gently sets me down, I feel a little weak in the knees. "Are you sure you can even walk, my dear?" He asks smirking.

"Oh, I can walk, stop making fun of me!" Alex laughs.

"Okay, I'll wait for you." I readjust my clothes and make my way towards castle doors.

I head towards the woods for remembering that James could literally be anywhere. 'There's no way I could let James wander alone at night, I need to find my answers tonight.' The woods were where I found him. So I decide to go that way, maybe I he is still waiting there.

I walk up to the edge of tree line, watching carefully. I spot James standing in the distance, his body language looks as if he is not alone.

I step closer and spot James talking to someone. I make my way towards them, watching my steps to make sure I'm not making any noise to alert them. I strain my ears to listen to what they're talking about.

"I don't know what you people want from me! You bought me here from my world and expect me to just know what to do here?"

"You're a useless, human. We brought you here for one job and you can't even do that right."

"What is the job!?"

"You idiot, you need to take Claire back to your world! As long as she is here, Alex's powers will be too strong. A love like this hasn't been in existence for the past 100 years and cannot be defeated. "She sighs. "For our master jack to take his rightful place on the throne, we need Alex and Claire to be broken apart."

'100 years?!' I stare at them in shock. I and Alex's bond being unbreakable makes the two of us stronger than I think.

"His love...? He loves her? And she loves him?"

"Yes. He has always loved her. She's been his since the moment she walked into this world. And even before she ever went to the human world."

"That bitch cheated on me! Who the hell is the Alex, I will destroy that bastard."

"Stop it, you're dumber than we thought."

I decide to remain quiet and not say anything, afraid that I may miss out on something important information if I start talking too soon. 'Oh my god is that?' Jack of all people emerges from the shadow, my eyes grow wide as I see him.

"If you knew this all along, why didn't you tell me?"

"Well, you never loved her, Jack, only her real love would be the rightful heir of the throne." Jack wilts, slightly nodding, looking defeated. He starts walking as if he will turn away.

I'm trying to find a covert way to follow them when, despite my best intentions, I crush a twig beneath my feet. I wince as all three of them turn to find me. 'Oh no! What did I just do?' I slowly stand up and reveal myself, the three of them gasp.

"How long has she been standing there!?"

"Long enough to understand my place here and what you three are doing. I'm no fool." I face Jack, confidently. "How can you expect yourself to become a ruler if you're unable to fight me? Why do you have to stoop so low?" Jack growls under his breath. "I have already shown you what a real ruler can do, haven't I?"

"Stop it! You know what I'm talking about!" James suddenly tugs on my arm. "Claire, listen to me." I spin around and glare at James. "Let! GO! OF! ME! RIGHT NOW!"

"Claire..." he drops my arm, as I instructed. "Please, Claire, this isn't our fight. Why do you even care what happens to these people anyway? They're all monsters, and this isn't our world."

I try my best to not snap at James, this is my real home and I will do everything to protect it. "I'm not leaving James, this is my home." James sighs and leans back, defeated.

"What a dumb human, you know she won't just go with you because you're begging her."

"Claire, you don't belong in this world. You know that. This isn't your home, no matter what you say."

"You must use some clever ways."

"What makes you think I'll go with him? What will you do?"

"I do, and you'll want to listen to all of it, sweetheart."

"Don't call me that Jack!" Jack snickers. "Ah, so feisty. I will miss that. You were the one who chose to leave this world eighteen years ago!"

'What? Why would I ever want to leave Night City? I'm sure there's more to the story that Jack isn't telling me.'

"You and Alex don't deserve to rule Night City. Not after you abandoned your people!"

"I'm sure I wouldn't have chosen to leave! That doesn't make any sense!"

"That's exactly what I thought, sweetheart but the truth is you did leave years ago. I would never leave my people like that."

"No of course not. You'd just enslave them and make this city miserable." Jack glares at me.

I look around until I find a wooden branch on the ground. I pick it up, rushing to stake Jack. Just then, I hear a familiar voice calling out to me. I turn to see Alex sprinting towards me as fast as he can. I stare at him full of confusion. "Alex! What are you doing here?" Alex gently takes me by the arms making me face him. "You aren't strong enough to take him down on your own, are you okay?" Jack screams in a rage and lunges at Alex before I can tell him anything.

Alex pushes me as Jack tackles him. The two are moving so fast in the darkness that I can't tell who is winning. "Alex!" I am about to run to him when I notice a shadow in the darkness. There is a glimmer of light coming off of the shadow, and I suddenly notice someone familiar casting spells. 'Dawn! She's here! I should have known. Her powers harbored by the witch will make us lose once again.'

I hear Alex screaming in pain, making my heart twist. Whatever Dawn is doing can't be helping Alex win. I need to stop her. I run as fast as I can and throw the ball of power. "AHH!" she screams and passes out on the ground.

"There's nowhere for you to go, Dawn. It's over"

I throw the magic towards Dawn. It takes her down, she holds at her chest like in severe pain.

"Bitch! First you took my love then you took over my city. You were never supposed to be back here! You were supposed to die with your useless parents in fire!"

"Dawn, how you knew my parents?"

"Not everyone liked them as rulers, bitch!" Anger consumes me, I harbor all my powers throwing them towards her, she flies before thudding on the ground, wounded. "It's over Dawn."

In the distance, I spot James trying to disappear in the portal to go back home. 'That coward, I'm glad he went back to the hole he crawled out from.'

I look over at Alex, panic in my chest. I'm afraid of what may happen to him with Jack, knowing that the fight would be dirty. I nearly jump for joy when I realize that Jack has also been knocked out. Dawn cries out as I snap my fingers, knocking her out with my magic once again. "Did we actually do this?"

"We did it! We won our battle, Claire, and all because of our love."

"I can't believe it."

"Let's put these two where they belong."

"They should be sentenced to death." Alex nods. "You're right, but for now..." he swoops me up in his arms and kisses me. "Help me with this!"

"What do you want me to do?"

"Chant the spell with me." I hold his hand, as he guides me through something. Both of us chant the same spell I read when I first got here. The power our love brings to us can take any which down. When the chant is over, the portal closes, leaving the two of us in dark. "Forever. Now you're stuck with me."

"This is my home!"

"Now, let's head back to the castle."

When I and Alex arrive, I see that the people of the city have gathered beneath the castle. Alex addresses his people. "Good people of Night City, the competition has been eliminated. You will now be take care of and safe for as long as you live!" the people cheer below us. I feel a joy spreading through me.

I step forward, and Alex steps back. "My people, I want to tell you how excited I am to be your ruler! Thank you for your trust and support in Alex and I. we promise we will do our best to make you proud! Long time ago, my parents were loved as rulers by all of you. Alex and I aspire to be like them. With your love and support, we'll make this city peaceful and harmonious to live in."

The cheers make me smile ear to ear. I wave and blow kisses to the adoring crowd.

Alex takes my hand, and before I know it, I'm back at the Castle in Alex's room. I'm standing between his legs, and he has his hands on my hips. Alex kisses my neck, then my lips. He looks at me. "What are you thinking about?"

"I know this is not the place to ask-"

"You're scaring me." Alex smiles, kissing the top of my head before he reaches the nightstand, pulling something out. "What are you doing?"

"Claire, my princess, will you give me the honor of becoming your husband?"

"Are you kidding me? I didn't knew people in the night city believed in the concept of marriage."

"Oh, we do! Now we're the rulers, our marriage will be the biggest celebration for years to come. What do you say? Would you want to take me as your husband?"

"Alex! Of course, yes! You are the prince charming I've always dreamt of."

Alex slips the extravagant ring in my finger before pulling me in his arms, kissing me passionately. "I love you."

"I can't wait for our happily ever after. I love you too Alex."

www.ingramcontent.com/pod-product-compliance
Lightning Source LLC
LaVergne TN
LVHW041609070526
838199LV00052B/3062